HEN

Hentoff, Nat

I'm really dragged
but nothing gets
me down

DATE			
AP 8 '75			
MAR 31 78			
MAY 28 79			
APR 3 96			

75-588

Hen

I'm really dragged
but nothing
gets me down

Also by Nat Hentoff

I'm really dragged but nothing gets me down

NAT HENTOFF

SIMON & SCHUSTER · NEW YORK

75-588

SBN: 671-65044-0 Trade
SBN: 671-65045-9 Library
Library of Congress Catalog Card Number: 68-29762
Manufactured in the United States of America
The Book Press Incorporated, Brattleboro, Vermont

6 7 8 9 10 11 12 13 14 15

1980

For

Jessica, Lisa, Mara, Miranda, Nicholas, Thomas—
and Cathy Schine

chapter 1

He was a tall guy, not too old, and he spoke easy. He looked, Jeremy thought, like one of those I'm-not-really-selling-anything-I'm-trying-to-help-you-out types on television. He would have been hard to figure for a minister with the brown suede jacket and those chukka boots.

The man moved closer to the mike. "Traditionally," he said, "the church has been a sanctuary. Now it will be again. I open my church to anyone resisting the draft. If there are arrests, the arrests will be in the church. And I and others past draft age will also be there to be arrested, for we support the resisters."

"Some sanctuary," Eric said, squinting at the sun. "So we all get busted together. Big deal. You know something? No one can take a bath for you, no one can die for you, and no one can get arrested for you. By the time I get that letter, Jeremy boy, I'm going to be the most conscientious student you ever saw. I'm not going into anybody's cage for five years. So what if he's in there with me? It's still five years out of *my* life."

Jeremy began to move back through the crowd. He broke into an open space as the minister suddenly shouted, "Conscription is for slaves, not for free men!" Jeremy sat down on a bench, Eric joining him.

"Maybe it'll be over in a year," Jeremy said.

Eric stretched out his long legs and looked up into the trees. "There'll always be another one for us. For a long time anyway. We were born in the wrong country. The thing to be now is Swiss or a Swede. Or a Canadian. Think about that. If you're born into the most powerful country in the world, you're screwed. When you've got power, you want to keep it, and that gets you into a lot of hassles."

"It doesn't bug you being able to stay in school while kids who can't make it or don't have the money get sent off?"

"Listen, if I was God, everybody would live forever and have everything he wants. And if I was president, I'd say to whatever country we were saving at the moment, 'Here's fifty billion dollars. Instead of putting it

8

in planes and bombs, we're just going to give it to you to get yourself together. Good luck, good-by, and drop us a line once in a while. You want some technical help, we'll be glad to send some people over. Unarmed.' "

"You didn't answer my question."

"Yes I did. What's the point of being bugged if you don't have any power to change anything? I'm certainly not going to volunteer. I got no quarrel with those people. So where does that leave me? Stay out of college and let them come get me so the army will be more democratic? That still makes me a killer, right? Hell, it could even get me killed. No, I'm not bugged the way you mean. Sure, I feel sorry for the poor bastards who don't have an out, but there's nothing I can do to help them without being phony and maybe suicidal. You remember what Kennedy said? 'Life is unfair.' Well, that's where it's at. You going to do any different?"

"No. It's a hell of a way to go to school, though, isn't it? One too many Fs, and it's your life."

"Yeah, but you can't beat that for an incentive. Man, are we ever going to be educated!"

"Do you ever think of dying, Eric? I mean, really, that you're going to die. I don't mean in a war, I mean naturally, normally."

"Hardly ever. There's a lot of time. There's a lot of time before you have to start thinking about that."

"I don't know, every once in a while it suddenly hits me and I can't shake it out of my mind for hours. I get scared as hell."

"You're all uptight because of this draft thing. Once

you get accepted somewhere, it'll ease off. And then, when you start, you'll be too busy to worry about that."

"I'm not so sure, not with *that* looking over my shoulder every time I take an exam."

"Then I guess you'll have to live with it. Right? You're making me feel spooky. Look, come by later. I got a new album. Three electronic sitars and a buzuki."

"Is it good?"

"I don't know yet. It's heavy, I'll tell you that."

Jeremy watched Eric lope across the park. The peace rally was still going on and Jeremy walked back to the edge of the crowd. An old man, his mouth hanging, his body in what seemed to be a permanent crouch, was talking to the backs of several young Negroes listening to the speeches. "Don't waste your time on those lib-lab fools, they don't know anything, they never knew anything. The only power that counts is in the barrel of a gun. Go in, go in, learn what they have to teach about killing, and then use it. You'll know where to use it." He chuckled thickly.

"You got it, old man," one of the Negroes turned around. "Yeah, you got it." He laughed. "Ain't he got it, little honky?"

"You talking to me?" Jeremy began to move away.

"Sure I am. Shouldn't I be talking to you?"

"Well, I don't dig killing. It's not my thing."

"Who said it was, little honky? You're in another bag. You a college boy, right?"

"I will be in the fall."

"Yeah. Yeah. Where you live, boy?"

"On the East Side."

"Where? Where on the East Side?"

"In the nineties."

"The number, I want the number."

"Why?"

"You don't want to give me the number where you live? You prejudiced or something?"

"I don't give strangers my address."

"Especially black strangers, huh, little honky? That's all right. We'll find you when we want you."

"Want me for what?"

"For whatever we want you for when we want you."

"Go in, go in," the old man was still croaking, "and steal the guns. Hide the guns. Get more guns and more guns."

The Negro grinned at him. "You are something else. I wish you was a brother. We don't have hardly any old brothers saying the truth. Ain't he something else, little honky?"

"He sure is."

Jeremy walked away fast, faster, until he was running. He looked around once. The Negro waved. Jeremy didn't wave back.

chapter 2

The door was closed, but the music came through. He would concede it was music in the sense that these days apparently any sound was music. Even no sound. At a concert a few years ago, the pianist had sat down and simply stayed there, not moving, for four minutes and thirty-three seconds. That was it. That was the composition—whatever noises were in the air while the man sat there. O.K., he could understand that. Whether it was a put-on or not, he could understand the principle, damn it. But this, this pounding from inside Jeremy's room, it was a pounding to get out at *him*, like an electronic beast slavering to devour the nearest adult. But how could an electronic beast slaver? Instead of saliva, there would be these jagged, crackling bursts of light. King Kong with an extension cord trailing behind.

"Hey, turn it DOWN!"

Silence. No compromise with *him*. Stubborn. Just plain stubborn. No, not plain. Hardly anything about his son was plain, was clear. God, he tried. He was willing to listen, but whenever they talked, the words never got anywhere. The words hung in the air, tangled in each other, until in frustration, one or the other, or both, would try to throw them, to shout them, with enough force so that they could penetrate. But it didn't work. Nothing worked.

He had wanted a son. Why had he wanted a son? Because that was one of the primal instincts, to perpetuate the race. Too abstract. Try again. He had wanted an extension of himself, someone with not only half his genes but with something of his values, his style, his life style, so that when he was gone, part of him would still be *there*, above ground, in the world. A shot at immortality. Too illusory. The way it's working out anyway. Try again. Well, at the least, he had wanted someone with whom he could share what he knew, someone he could help avoid the more obvious mistakes. Sure, you have to get hurt to grow up, but you don't have to get unnecessarily hurt, stupidly hurt, not if there's someone around who knows *that* part of the score, who's *been* there. Here he was with a legacy of information to pass on, but his heir was renouncing all rights of succession. Why? Why wouldn't he *listen* to him? Why wouldn't he learn from him?

The door opened, and there he was, his mouth set, his son, the familiar stranger.

"Look," said Jeremy, "if you can't listen to this music with the volume up, you're not getting it. It's *meant* to be loud. Loudness is *part* of it. It's not listening *to*, it's listening from inside. You have to go all the way inside until there's just you and the music, like in a space capsule."

"But you're not living in your own space capsule. You're living here with us."

"Oh damn it, it wasn't that loud anyway."

"Why don't you use those earphones?"

"That's not the same as having the whole room turn into sound. Earphones compress the music, they compress me. The whole idea of rock is to break out of yourself. I mean expand yourself, not turn yourself into a little ball."

"Well, I'm afraid you're going to have to control your expansion until you have your own apartment. When you're living with other people, there are certain compromises you have to make. It's elementary civil liberties, Jeremy. I have the right not to be assaulted by your music."

"What's the use? O.K., O.K., you win again. I kept it down and it's still not enough. Nothing is ever enough."

Jeremy ran into the room, rushed back with a record

in his hands, and with much hard breathing finally cracked it in two. You could be much more dramatic, Sam thought, with those old 78s.

"Now that's stupid!"

"It's over, it's over. Don't you understand. You've won! Enjoy the silence. Dig the silence. I'm going over to Eric's. The civil liberties are more equally distributed over there."

"I didn't say you could go out. And after this tantrum—"

Jeremy went back into his room and slammed the door. Now the silence behind that door was like a thing, a lump of spite. The father stood, feeling his heart pound, pound to get out, to get out at whom? At what? There was a beast inside him in the clotted silence, a nonelectronic beast, give it that much credit. That's how Stalin killed Lenin. He knew Lenin had high blood pressure and he made him angrier and angrier until he killed him. I wanted a son, the father stared at the door, and I got my assassin.

chapter 3

"Grass is less harmful—"
"Than liquor."
"Grass is less harmful—"
"Than straight cigarettes."
"Grass is—"
"Nonaddictive."
"Then why the hell don't you take some?"
"Because you left out one big fat part of the cate-chism. Grass—"

"Can get you busted."

"Yeah. Look, Peter, how do I know what kind of job I'm going to be applying for some day? And my ticket comes back from the Supercomputer—canceled. Eric Greenfield, busted for possession. Discard that man. No, no, you can't be too careful. Like how do I know you're not a nark, working up your college tuition through the special incentive program of the Federal Bureau of Narcotics?"

"As a matter of fact," Peter said solemnly, "and I'll tell you because you won't believe it—and that's the best cover you can get—I'm an apprentice for the C.I.A. We get a quota of subversives, actual and potential, to send in each month. And if we make it for a year, we get tenure in the junior division plus a full scholarship, *plus* a guaranteed love potion their chemical division has developed that'll turn any girl you want into an absolute, total love slave."

Clowns. Jeremy watched Eric and Peter rapping, and saw clowns. A long, thin clown and a round, soft clown. He got up for another slice of pizza and saw himself stretched on the ground, his head in some spade soldier's lap, waiting for the helicopter. "Easy, man, easy, you'll be O.K." But how did I get here? "You flunked out, man, don't you remember? Came exam time and you went blank. You must have wanted to be here all the time, helping all us disadvantaged cats win the war. You a good little honk. You hurry up and get yourself together, you hear, and come back here with us, and do your thing for your country. I'm going to put you in, boy, I'm going to put you in for honorary soul brother."

"Hey, Jeremy," Eric called after him, "you going into that tutorial thing? Now that it's in the school, there's no hassle. I mean, you don't have to go walking around *their* streets. And it looks good on your record, you know, helping your fellow man and all that."

"You started?"

"Yeah. I expected some big, tough spade ready to break me in two if I didn't make him as smart as me in one hour flat. But this thin little thirteen-year-old comes sliding in, so polite and shy. You know something? After we got into it, and I began showing him things nobody had ever made clear to him before, we got along just fine. That kid's got a good head. All he needed was some fundamentals. Jesus, what do they *do* in those schools?"

"Some of those kids are supposed to be disturbed, aren't they?" Jeremy asked.

"Oh, disturbed. What does that mean? Christ, we don't have disturbed kids in our class? Sarah dropping acid on weekends, and this head here?"

"You're like a premature parent, you know that?" Peter scowled. "What you don't know, you put down. Grass makes me feel good. That classifies me as disturbed? Listen, the time is now. O.K., acid maybe's something else. In its present stage, mind you. There'll be safe acid before long. But grass, why, you got to be disturbed *not* to take grass. Listen, the whole world's a head shop. It depends on what kind of head you want to be. You can be a straight American head, sleeping pills,

Scotch, all those traditional ways of cutting off the high frequencies. You ever realize that? The old folks go off on lows, not highs. Anyway you can also be a part-time new American head. That's going to be my bag. You do what you have to do during the week, and you fly through the weekend. Or you can be an out-of-control head, which is where Sarah-in-the-sky-with-diamonds is going. Or you can be a revolutionary head, like Mike. Tear down that old corporate liberalism! Build the new society! Heads up for participatory democracy! That's a high too. Not mine, but what the hell, it's like buying a sweater. You pick your own style."

"Suppose you don't know yet what your style is?" said Jeremy.

"Then shop around. Want some grass?"

"That's all I need. My father finds me holding, and I'm a prisoner for a month."

"Why does he have to find it?"

"Because he will. That's the kind of head I am. I always get caught, a real punishment head. Explain me that."

"You're a good boy, Jeremy, poor boy." Peter looked at him sadly. "They already got you in shape. A few rough edges maybe, but you're almost dead and gone. I dunno. You think there's any hope for this young man, Eric?"

"Why ask me? I'm like him."

"No, you're not. You are something else. Who knows what you do in the dark? But this one, dark and light is all the same to him. He just worries."

"Give me some of that grass." Jeremy held out his hand.

"Well, how about that? This young man is coming into his own."

"Oh, I'm not going to smoke it."

"Then what do you want it for?"

"A status symbol, O guru, while I contemplate the possibility of not being me."

chapter 4

"How was the movie?"

"O.K. A little slow, but there was some groovy lighting."

"Didn't it seem artificial to you, his dying at the end?"

"I didn't think about it. I just accepted it."

"He didn't die at the end, you goddamn liar. Where were you?"

"Oh Jesus."

"WHERE WERE YOU?"

"Just walking, looking into a couple of button shops, looking at some new records."

"With whom?"

"I don't have to tell you with whom."

"You damn well do have to tell me. So long as you're living in this house, you are accountable to me. Turn out your pockets."

"Who do you think you are, the F.B.I.? Let's see your warrant."

"Don't get flip with me. Turn out your pockets."

"I swallowed it all, pot, acid, STP, Speed, all in one big, glorious gulp. You'll have to take me to the hospital and have me pumped."

"Don't think I wouldn't do it."

"Oh you'd do it. If you weren't afraid of being busted for child abuse, you'd have me stick my hand in the oven to prove my innocence by not getting burned."

"I've had it with you. I am responsible for you and therefore you are responsible to me."

"O.K. Let me relieve you of that burden."

And out went his son, weightless. But he, the rejected father, stood, eyes popping, fists clenched, heavy with the lump of injustice in him. All the tension all day, every day, selling, selling, you need a full page, a quarter-of-a-page doesn't do justice to that product. Why hide what you've developed? Pressing, clear, cool, full of facts, full of concern, and real concern. He was not a pimp or a whore, he would never urge any company to overextend itself, that's why he was able to get in to see anybody. Anybody knew Sam Wolf was straight. Anybody knew Sam Wolf had the knowledge of chemical engineering to edit the magazine himself, but selling was where the action was, the challenge, the money. And straight money. He earned it, the magazine earned it. And at the end of the day, what did he get for it? To come home to be deviled by a kid who doesn't know anything, who takes the food his father gives him and the clothes his father gives him and goes to the school his father pays for, and wishes his father would drop dead. That, Sam knew with sudden, utter conviction, would be the best thing for that boy. That would teach him something. What would he do then? The insurance would keep them in the apartment and eating, but where would the records come from and the hi-fi equipment and the money for college? He'd have to cut off all that damn hair and get a job. Yes, if he dropped dead, that would shake the boy into reality. My God, what was he thinking? That kid can drive you out of your mind.

Lillian came into the room. "What was that all about?"

"He walked out. Just like that. He didn't go to any movie, and when I caught him in a lie, his only answer was to walk out. That's some character your son has."

"Sam, it's late. You can't let him walk the streets."

"He'll be back. You don't have to worry about Jeremy. He's full of talk, just so long as it doesn't cost him anything. He'll get tired, he'll be back. I should lock the door, that's what I should do. Let him learn something."

"Sam, you're going to drive him out for good. You know how stubborn he is."

"Where? Where would he go? With what money?

Oh no, that boy is stuck here. And we're stuck with him."

"Why are you after him all the time? He does well enough in school. All right, he's disrespectful, I suppose, and he walks around looking like a sheep dog, but they're all like that. He'll get over it."

"I don't give a damn what they're all like. I'm not the father of the lot of them, thank God. But in my own house I will not have a liar, a slob, a snotty kid. Would *your* father have permitted that kind of behavior? Would mine? Don't tell me about the times changing. What's right is right. That kid is going to shape up."

"And if he doesn't?"

"I haven't done this well by accepting the possibility of failure. If I can't handle my own kid, how can I handle anything? You think I'm going to let myself be taken by my own kid? Who the hell does he think he is?"

"Maybe he's trying to find out."

"You're talking like one of those articles in the ladies' magazines. All right, let him find out, but in the right way."

chapter 5

It looked like her, that straight back and straight blonde hair and swift, cutting stride. God, she was something, if that was her. Cool, so cool on the outside, eyes mocking, light my fire, but how? He had never been able to look straight into those eyes for long, he'd end up stammering at his hands or her books or saying nothing, grinning like a retarded child. Jeremy ran to catch up, and touched her shoulder.

"Tracy."

She whirled around, and laughed.

"Oh, it's you. Good thing you called my name." She opened her hand and showed him a handkerchief with some dark grains of something in it. "Pepper. Robbie's idea. He learned it from a jazz musician who got mugged once and didn't have faith in learning judo. He said how do you know the other guy doesn't know judo better."

Robbie. Jeremy's face got tight. Robbie, a dolt with an electric guitar. If the power failed, all that's left is a dolt. He knew they went out together, but what did they talk about? Well, if you've got that thing, I suppose it doesn't matter. Jeremy risked looking straight at her. There was nothing there, not even a teasing light, just plain old friendliness. He could just as well have been a well-mannered talking dog. What if he put his arm around her? She'd laugh, and maybe even let it stay there, but so what? It wasn't favors he needed.

"You can withdraw your weapon. I'll walk you where you're going."

"Why, thank you, Jeremy. But I'm a little early. Hey, why don't we look into the free show down there? If you're not in a hurry."

Two blocks away, at the corner of Sixth Avenue and Eighth Street, as always on a weekend night, there were bunches of people arguing. An open air forum for anybody who wanted to argue any side of any question, or make one up.

As they came up to the clumps of debates, a loud, hoarse voice from near the center drew them in. "Nothing personal, you understand. I want to make sure you understand that. But you people—not *you* necessarily, you might be an investment banker, for all I know—but the *mass* of Negroes are so hung up on color that you keep running around in circles. First it's all you out there are racists and that's why I'm where I am. Then it's black is beautiful and where I am is going to be the best damn place in the city. And then it's all you racists out there better give us the money to make this the best damn place in the city or else we'll burn down where we are. I mean it's like a clown show. No offense. I'm talking sociology, not personalities. Only when you realize it's the *system* that keeps you down will you go beyond color into the nitty-gritty, the cancer of capitalism."

Jeremy and Tracy had squeezed through the crowd and saw a short, muscular, bald man in his fifties who was looking up at a tall, skinny young Negro.

"All right now, you finished? You finished taking our words, too? What do you know about nitty-gritty? What do you know about the brother? Man, what do you know about anything? System! I don't care what it's called, capitalism or socialism or communism, it's always racism. You think it's a clown show, huh? Well, man, you're going to find some clowns with guns and bombs and plastique right where you are at. The blood is rising, man, and unless there are *big* changes very soon —and I don't see any big changes coming—you're going to see some circus. You'll die laughing. Yes, indeed, you will BREAK UP."

"Oh God," Tracy said, "they're both so full of it."

"Well, he's right, you know." Jeremy carefully put his hand on her elbow. "There'll be more violence."

"Oh, that's not what I mean. God, they're all so *predictable*. It's like most of the people you see have been programmed. You push a button and all those words come out and they don't mean anything because they don't come from anywhere that means anything. They get so excited, as if they've thought up something all new, but all they're saying is what everybody else who's been programmed that way is saying."

The bald white man was smiling. "Talk, talk, talk. That guerrilla warfare only works, friend, when you're in the majority. You carry guns or bombs into white neighborhoods and—WHOOSH!—you'll be in ghettos from the Middle Ages then, with high-rise walls and round-the-clock guards."

"Listen, Jeremy," Tracy turned from the debate, "I've got to go. I told Robbie I'd meet him at eleven. It's just up the street. You don't have to walk me."

He watched her stride to the corner. The tall, skinny Negro brushed past him, muttering, "Waste of time, waste of time. They just can't learn." Jeremy wanted to say he'd like to learn, at least he'd like to let the man know he agreed with him that it *is* a racist society. But what was the point? That guy didn't need any favors either.

chapter 6

Hearing the key in the lock, he looked at his watch. 12:30. The boy couldn't even put up a good show of leaving home.

"Changed your mind?"

"O.K. O.K. Why don't you just let me go to bed?"

"You think it's that simple. You lie to me, then you slam out of here and no more's to be said about it?"

"What is it you want? You want me to leave?"

"I want you to show me the respect of not lying to

me. What kind of relationship can we have if it's not based on trust? Have I ever given you reason not to trust me? Have I ever said I would get you something, and then not gotten it? When a bill comes from the school, you don't have to worry about it, you know it'll be paid."

"God, that's all trust is to you, keeping that kind of promise and paying bills?"

"All right, if that definition doesn't suit you, what does?"

"How do I say it? How do I say it so you'll have any idea of what I'm talking about? Look, where it's at is you don't trust *me*. Like you've got your list, people I'm not allowed to see."

"You know why you can't see them. I will not have you hanging around with potheads and other kinds of drug takers. Nor will I have you associate with any of those so-called revolutionaries. Do you know what it'll mean to your career if there's a file on you as being some kind of subversive? Listen, I know something about how government security agencies operate. Pictures are being taken all the time at all those demonstrations. And lists are being compiled all the time of people who go to certain kinds of meetings and subscribe to certain kinds of publications. I'm not saying I'm in favor of all that, but that's what's going on, and it's going to keep going on. If you want to get somewhere, you've got to stay clean. It's not even as if you were old enough to have any strong beliefs about politics. Why get yourself in trouble when you don't even know what it's all about?"

"How do you know I don't know what it's all about? I know some things very clearly. That this country talks about peace and makes war. That this country talks about freedom but tries to run things wherever it can. That this country is hated all over the world, and especially by young people all over the world."

"Listen, I'm not going to engage in a discussion of American foreign policy with you. That's not the point. The point is that if you don't agree with it, and you want to change it, you have to get into a position in this society where you pull some weight, where people will listen to you and not think you're some kind of kook."

"All right, you're respectable. You've got a position in the society. So why aren't you trying to change anything?"

"Because." Should he level with him? Did he have a choice? "Because I don't think anything can really be changed, not basically. When I was your age, and for a little longer, I used to think socialism was the answer. Everyone would share in the decision making, everyone would share the wealth. Well, I've found that most people don't want to make decisions, even if they had the power. Most people like to be told what to do. They want order and security, not power. And they certainly don't want to share *anything*. Most people are like pack rats. They spend their lives collecting. A wife, children, furniture, cars, television sets. That's what makes them happy. Well, if not happy, at least it gives them a sense of belonging somewhere. That's the way it is. That's the way I am. Maybe you'll be different. A few are. But if you want to be different for a purpose that isn't just self-gratification, you've got to earn enough respect so that people will pay attention."

"But you say there's no point anyway, that nothing can basically be changed. So what does respectability have to do with going your own way?"

"Maybe I'm wrong. Maybe change is possible. If things get bad enough. If the machines really do take over and make a lot of people superfluous unless there is change. All I'm saying is, if I'm wrong, if there *is* going to be a role for people with different ideas and different values, they'll still have to be able to communicate with the average man. And the average man isn't going to listen to someone who looks weird or has a bad record. I can't tell you what to do with your life, but I'm trying to show you how not to waste it, whichever way you go."

"Yeah. Well, thanks."

Jeremy went into his room, and the music started. Too loud, but what the hell, he came home. And the boy listened to what he had to say for a little while anyway. The father poured himself a drink. And added to the glass. Maybe he shouldn't have said that. How can a kid look up to a father who calls most people pack rats? But the truth is the truth. He remembered the steps, in Brownsville, on which he and Hershey sat for hours, talking, past midnight, past one o'clock. About politics, about ending the profit system, about the new America in which you could be prosperous without being guilty because there would be no lower class and prosperity would be measured by the riches of the spirit and the intellect. And now Hershey was a management consultant and he, today he had signed a new ad schedule with the company that makes napalm. Only one of its products, and one of the least important, so far as its profits are concerned, but it is one. Truth is truth. If he didn't take the ads, what difference would that make? It would make him a fool, a fool who might be temporarily applauded by his son. But a fool. Would he be an accomplice when that napalm scorched some child? Everybody who pays taxes is an accomplice, and if you don't pay them, the government will get them anyway. He could have told Jeremy more about how impossible it was to change the system, to change people, in any significant way. But he'd told him enough to answer the question. He fantasied himself picketing his own magazine because it carried ads from the manufacturer of napalm, and he laughed.

"What's so funny?" his wife asked him when he came into the bedroom. "I dozed off. Is Jeremy back? Oh yes, I hear. Is he all right?"

"Yes, he's all right. He's as good as he'll ever be. He can only go downhill from here."

"Whatever are you talking about?"

"I thought you wanted to know what was funny."

"Yes, what was?"

"Nothing."

chapter 7

"The fruits of corporation law," his father said. Because of the tone, dry and nasty, Jeremy assumed he was supposed to make some kind of comment. The worldly-wise-father-instructing-his son tone it was. Jeremy looked out the window as they came up the drive.

"He owns all this, huh? All those trees, all this land?"

"Yes, sir, the fruits of a lifetime of dedicated skill for them what already have more than they know what to do with." His father didn't seem to be answering him.

Jeremy had picked up the wrong signal. This perform-
ance was for his mother.

"What are you trying to say, that Jack is a crook?
That he didn't earn this?"

"Who said crook? I'm sure he's never done anything
that hasn't been entirely within the law. Sometimes a
micromillimeter within the law, but what the hell, he and
his clients have a great deal to do with making the laws
anyway."

"Why aren't you honest about it?" His mother's voice
had that ugly edge now that made Jeremy dread the
ride home. "It's not what he does you don't like, it's him
you can't stand."

"How to tell the dancer from the dance?" A cop
waved the car toward a nearby field that had been
turned into a parking space for the night. "My, my,
when did he buy the local police force?"

"The man is probably off duty, earning a little extra
money. They don't pay them much in a small town like
this. Why *do* you dislike Jack so. I never could understand it."

His father leaned out the window. "Tell me, officer,
why the presence of the police?"

"I go where I'm told, sir. Plenty of room over there."

"Off duty, hell. Just an extra service for the lord of the
manor."

"That *is* what bothers you, isn't it, that Jack's a big
man?"

"Oh he has the trappings, but it depends on what you
mean by big. Big, like will he go down in history? Big,

like will he be missed when he's gone? Or simply big in the belly, big in the head, and big in the stock market?"

"I see, the simple man of virtue is making a moral judgment. How did you become so pure all of a sudden? Is this a sudden religious conversion? Did you see someone I didn't see on the road? Was that Damascus we just passed? I thought it was White Plains."

Jeremy sighed. The insult match was on again. Maybe he ought to volunteer to keep score. What a way to waste Sunday. Because her crummy brother had a twenty-fifth wedding anniversary, he was up here, caught in a cross-fire in a battle that had nothing to do with him. Talk about innocent bystanders.

There was his uncle at the door of the house. He was sure enough big. Jeremy wondered what it was like to be inside all that flesh, to carry all of it around. To be that old. Sixty or something he was. How often did he think about dying? Did he think? What kind of mind do you have when you're that old and fat? It must be like a turntable going at 16 r.p.m. His uncle came toward them, smiling. Out of the car, his mother gave him her cheek to kiss. And his father shook his hand.

"Lillian, you look marvelous. And Sam, I don't know how you do it. It must be all that tennis."

His father was smiling too. The rules of the game. Tell him like it is, Dad. Jeremy extended a limp hand. Tell him he's a malefactor of great wealth. No, that's obsolete. Jeremy looked at his uncle's buckled black shoes. You, sir, are the legal arm of the military-industrial complex. And if you're lucky, you'll die before the court convenes again at Nuremberg. It's gonna happen, Mike said, all the fat cats will be brought before a world court for crimes in Asia, for crimes in Latin America. Fat chance. My uncle will die choking on a piece of the best steak.

"What a solemn young man you are. What's new, Jeremy?"

"Nothing much."

"Picked your college yet?"

"I've picked several, but none of them has picked me yet."

"Let's talk about that later. I know some people."

I bet you do. Jeremy looked at the cold blue eyes and immediately looked away. Were they cold, or did he just think them cold? They were cold. But then so were his right now. He hoped they were. I'm not about to take any favors from you, Uncle Jack. Still, Jeremy couldn't help wondering, did he know anyone at Columbia?

They all went into the house, his parents and the malefactor. Jeremy walked off to the right toward a large, smooth clearing with a swimming pool at one side and a small pond at the other. On long tables were arrays of hors d'oeuvres and, for God's sake, shrimp trees. Tiers of shrimps arranged like small firs. Large ladies and scrawny ladies and men who all looked pretty much alike—some with glasses, some without—pawed at the triangles of smoked salmon, skewered the meat balls, plucked from the dead sea tree, all the while jabbering at each other. A few feet away from the food tables was a table set up as a bar with a Negro in a white coat. Take the stone grinning jockey off the lawn and put him behind a bar. But this one wasn't grinning. He was young, cool, safe inside his head while his fingers did what had to be done. And did it well. Jeremy envied him, certain he was hating all these whiteys, him too. That must feel good, knowing absolutely where you are and where they are, the enemy. They have nothing to do with me either, Jeremy was talking in his head to the black young man behind the bar. But you don't care about that, do you? Well, no reason you should. Nothing I can do for you, and nothing you can do for me.

"Jeremy, I hardly recognized you. Why don't we see more of you?"

She was about as big as Uncle Jack, but firmer, harder. With a smile on, she looked like an alligator. Imagine being married to that for twenty-five years, lying in bed next to it, seeing it every morning and every night, and taking trips with it. How do people get themselves trapped that way? But maybe he likes her. That's even worse. To think that's possible. And if it is, it could happen to him. Impossible.

"Well, I've—" But she was being kissed and congratulated on the other side of the shrimp tree.

"Young man." A tall, thin person, with white hair and what he probably intended to be a smile, pointed a celery stalk at Jeremy. "How do you justify that hair?"

"I don't justify it, I wear it."

"I'm not baiting you, young man. I'm curious as to why you feel the need to wear it that way."

"Jeremy," his uncle manifested himself with a large

hand on his shoulder, "this is Bill McDermott. Don't let him intimidate you, he's our district attorney."

"I was just asking this young fellow why he felt called upon to deprive the barbering profession of their livelihood."

What *was* this? Jeremy felt his face burn. He was an exhibit, genus American teenager. Who the hell did they think they were?

"Well, as it happens," Jeremy looked off into the darkening sky, "this has become an article of religious faith to me. We are taught that hair is the avatar of the life force. I mean, look at all the generals. Did you ever see one with long hair? And all the murderers, especially the psychopaths, are practically compulsive about haircuts. It's an established fact, you know, the most grucsome crimes of the present day have invariably been committed by people with very short hair. That's one of the main reasons for the high rate of recidivism. Prisons keep feeding into that short hair syndrome."

"All right, kid, I don't like being put on," the tall, thin person looked at him hard. Jeremy felt like putting his hands out for the cuffs that were in old Bill McDermott's head. You can't bust me, because my uncle would bust you.

"Gee, I'm sorry you took it that way, sir. But that is what we are taught."

"By whom?" His uncle's look was sour.

"Well, we don't know his true name, but he appears to us from time to time when his band comes through town. He's called The Amplifier."

His uncle shook his head more in anger than in sorrow, took McDermott by the elbow, and left Jeremy to feel good.

Some time later, as Jeremy was hiding a meat ball in the shrimp tree, he saw McDermott and a billowy lady, their backs turned, on the way to the table with the drinks.

"That little snot-nosed Jew," the district attorney was saying. "You can be damned sure he'll get out of the draft."

"Sh-h-h," said the lady. "You wouldn't want *them* to hear you talk like that."

Jeremy ducked underneath the food table, made a megaphone with his hands, and droned, "Beware, McDermott, beware of the infidel. He will suck your soul dry-y-y."

chapter 8

He hadn't been in the school for more than two years. He just didn't have time for parents' meetings, and Lillian took care of the individual meetings with the home room teacher. But this time the letter had asked that both of them come. Four in the afternoon—that blew at least two calls he could have made. He felt uncomfortable in this building because he was still uncomfortable about sending the boy to a private school. After all these years, he wasn't sure it had been the right thing to do. Not only because of the money, although that bothered him. Here he was, paying taxes, entitled to free education for his son, but spending nearly two thousand dollars a year in this place.

"He's a shy, sensitive child," Lillian had said, "and he'll be lost in those big classes in the public school. Besides, you know as well as I do, with more and more Puerto Ricans coming in and with the Negro children coming from the homes they do, he'll be held down in those classes." They've got advanced classes for the smart ones, he'd said. "Yes," Lillian had persisted, "but they're big classes, and how long can they be that advanced when more and more of the others are always coming into the school system? Standards *have* to go down all the way down the line. Listen, I'm for equal opportunity and all that, but are you going to sacrifice your own son just to be able to say you've kept him in the public school with the colored and the Puerto Ricans? Just to say *you* haven't run away, when *he's* the one who has to pay for your act of principle. Besides"—and this is what had really got him—"it'll be a lot easier for Jeremy to get into a good college from one of the better private schools." All right, all right. That he couldn't argue with.

Still, he was uncomfortable. Sam Wolf, who used to talk about the classless society, is helping to make the lines tighter. But what can you do? Truth is truth. They came to the room, 417, and Sam knocked. A short, bulky, bearded man, who looked to be in his early thirties, opened the door. Jeremy had never said his teacher had a beard. It wasn't precisely the right example to set for a young boy, Sam thought, while acknowledging that at least the beard was neatly trimmed. He'd had a beard once, just for a summer, and given a choice, he probably would have kept it. No time and blood wasted shaving, and he'd liked what it had done for his face, hiding his blurred chin. But he had not had a choice. No one would have hired him with a beard. You put off a sales prospect by looking too different. He begins to wonder about how solid you are and then he begins to wonder how solid what you're selling is. No, a beard is no way to build confidence. Not in the real world anyway. It's O.K. for young people and for certain professions, Sam supposed, but essentially it's an affectation. A pretense. A pretense of being different. And underneath, the ones with the beards, the ones who kept them when they grew up, they worried about the same things he did.

"Sam, this is Mr. O'Connor." Lillian was always the hostess. They shook hands, and Sam waited for the new worry he was about to get.

"I appreciate your having come," O'Connor said, waving them to chairs near his desk. "I've been somewhat concerned about Jeremy these last few months."

"I thought his grades were good," Sam broke in.

"Oh yes, he does the work, and he's moderately conscientious about it. But he seems, well, removed. Abstracted. He used to be a very active participant in class discussions, but these days he has to be practically dragged in."

"Is this going to affect the report you write on him

for college?" Lillian was trying to be matter-of-fact, but Sam saw her hands tremble and was ashamed. Why was he ashamed? He didn't know exactly, but he was ashamed.

O'Connor raised his eyebrows. "I hadn't even thought about that. No, these days I write warm recommendations about all our young men."

"If they all get good recommendations," Sam said, trying to smooth out his annoyance, "what's the point of anyone working harder than anyone else?"

"In the first place," O'Connor leaned back in his chair, "the point of what we do here, as I thought you knew, is to encourage the students to learn because they want to learn, not to compete with each other. But I'm not being entirely honest in answer to what you were really asking. Is it fair to be equally enthusiastic about all of them? Well, I'm not. Some recommendations are warmer than others, but they all do get recommended, even though some, I expect, are going to have a hard time where they insist they want to go. But if I can't convince them to try a less exacting college, I'll try to help them get in anyway. I will not bear the responsibility of sending someone I know into the army. At the same time, of course, I am thereby responsible for someone I don't know, probably some black kid, going in. That's why I'm leaving here when the year is up. I'm going to teach in public school, in East Harlem. It won't change the odds by more than the tiniest fraction, if that, but there are colleges looking for the disadvantaged —isn't that a charming euphemism?—and I'm going to help them find some."

"That's very commendable, I'm sure." Sam was getting to dislike this man with the beard more and more. "But about Jeremy."

"That's what I wanted to ask you. Is there any trouble at home?"

"I wouldn't know," said Sam. "We are not communicating very well."

"He doesn't talk very much at home," Lillian now had her hands clasped tightly, "but I thought that was just a stage they all go through. But he doesn't seem depressed or anything like that. A little—what you said—abstracted.

"I have the feeling," said O'Connor, "that something is bothering him a great deal, something he may not even be able to define very precisely himself." He smiled at Sam. "I haven't been communicating very well with him either. Although we used to. I know this sounds like a vague reason for asking you to come, but I thought you might have some more information or understanding of why he's become so—so flat. He's just there now. He just doesn't react except to do what he has to do." 95-588

"You think he needs treatment?" Sam asked grimly.

"I'm somewhat of a renegade on that subject. I think there are ills of the spirit that may be made only worse by a psychologist or psychiatrist poking around—particularly in an adolescent's head. That way you can create distortions where before there were just questions. No, he doesn't need treatment. I expect this will pass in time. I just thought there might be a missing piece of the puzzle at home. I don't want to worry you. There's nothing in the least to be alarmed about. It's just that the boy seems unhappy, in a curiously unfocused kind of way."

"That may not be a bad thing," Sam said. "Learning to be unhappy, and learning you survive it."

"Practice makes perfect?" O'Connor looked at him. It was, Sam felt, a distinctly patronizing look.

"You live in a state of constant euphoria?" Sam ignored a warning glare from Lillian.

"Alas, no. But I don't think I'm ennobled by the times I am unhappy."

"I'm not talking about ennobling, I'm talking about toughening."

"Ah yes, well, Jeremy isn't toughened yet by any means, but would you really want him to be? You lose a lot in the process—spontaneity, openness, trust."

"I want him to survive," Sam said brusquely, and rose.

"Yes," O'Connor also got up, "but there are different ways of surviving."

"Mr. O'Connor," Lillian moved toward him, "it was very thoughtful of you to bring this to our attention, and we will try to get Jeremy to open up more."

"You may not be able to," O'Connor said. "Don't press it. Actually I probably shouldn't have taken your time. But I confess I did want to meet Jeremy's father."

"And your verdict?" Sam was not smiling.

"I'm delighted to have met you, Mr. Wolf."

"You think I'm insufficiently idealistic."

"It's our common condition. We all do want to survive."

Sam and Lillian, going down the stairs, were silent. "You think," she finally said, "he'll write a good report?"

"Sure. He's weak. Like he said, he wouldn't want to have to imagine Jeremy's head being blown off in some rice paddy."

"And that's weakness?"

"Look at things as they are, Lillian. If everybody were like that, or if a lot of people were like that, whom would you get in the army? And if you don't have an army, you're weak. Weakness leads to weakness. Would I do the same thing if I were in his place? Probably. But I'd know I was being weak. I wouldn't call it idealism."

"He didn't use that word, you did."

"I'm sure that's the way he thinks of himself. Like his going off to a slum school. What it amounts to is that he's like a hemophiliac when it comes to guilt. It keeps flowing, and he's not strong enough to live with a lot of it, so he keeps trying to reduce it to manageable proportions."

"I really don't know what you're talking about, as if you can tell so much about a person in just a few minutes."

"That's my game, Lillian, sizing people up."

"Well, I do hope he writes a good report. Maybe we ought to invite him to dinner one night."

"Better yet, I'll send him a case of Scotch for Christmas, like my father used to with the Internal Revenue man."

"You can't be serious, you wouldn't be so crass."

"No, I'm on a different level now. On this level, what you buy, you buy much more subtly. One way or another, every boy in this school is going to college. That's why your worrying about what kind of report he'll write is a waste of energy. We are the ruling class, Lillian. Well, not the ruling class, but members of the aristocracy. Don't you feel aristocratic?"

"The trouble with Jeremy is that he has a father who doesn't know what he wants."

"I'm too old to have an identity problem that anyone should care about. Concentrate on the boy, Lillian. Lay off me."

"With pleasure."

They rode home in silence. Sam fantasied O'Connor coming to him for a job. "First thing, the beard comes off. Second thing, you apologize." "For what?" "For considering yourself superior to me." As O'Connor apologized, Sam nodded in satisfaction.

chapter 9

You wouldn't take Mike, just looking at him, for a
Noble Soul. First of all, he doesn't look it, chunky as he
is, and laughing as much as he does. And besides liking
to eat, he smokes grass once in a while, and falls in love
every other week, it seems.

"Why don't you admit it?" Eric was saying. "You
have no discrimination. Nobody who gets a hard-on as
easily as you has any *taste*. With you it's all *appetite*."

"Now that's interesting," Mike said. "See what's happened to a word. Taste, the way you use it, the way almost everybody uses it, means a narrowing, a refining. Of what? Of appetite. But once you get into that bag you get an image of yourself you have to keep protecting. You've got to be on guard—if I dig this and show it, do I look like I have less taste than I had before? So the Beatles groove me—but only starting with *Rubber Soul* is the way it's supposed to be now. But I still have an appetite for the early things they did. Simple stuff. 'I Want to Hold Your Hand.' So I'm not discriminating enough, my taste hasn't *evolved* enough. So what? Why does it *matter* to anybody but me what I like? Because everybody watches everybody else to make sure his own taste is the *right* taste. And if somebody's out of line, you've got to put him down so you can stay up."

"What does all that have to do," Eric poked a finger at him, "with how quickly you get turned on by so many different girls?"

"Because," Mike grinned, "I have a big, healthy appetite and a lot of curiosity. Why should I hold down either?"

"You might just as well be an animal then. Right?"

"Well, I am, same as you. The difference between us is, I'm not worried about it."

Jeremy frowned. "But surely you wouldn't sleep with just anyone."

"Of course not. I have tastes in girls like I have in everything else, but they're not narrow. And I don't try to keep them narrow. If I don't try them all out now, when am I going to do it? It can get awfully damn complicated if you start experimenting too late. My father's been married four times, you know. What a mess he's in, with all the money he has to make for all the families, and the way he has to split his time so he can spread his attention around to all his different whelps. That's because he didn't sleep with anybody until he was like twenty-two, and then as soon as he did, he married her. And he got into the habit. With him, it was never a question of adultery. Once he made it with somebody, he had to get rid of the one before. And that was because he'd held in his sexual appetite so long its importance got all out of proportion."

"I still don't see what this has to do with having some *taste*," Eric said.

"Why are you in such a hurry to have good taste? Because that's what you mean, *good* taste. Why not follow your appetites in anything until you've had enough experience to really know what you like? And to hell with what anybody else thinks about it. They're not living *your* life."

"What you're advocating is just plain self-indulgence." Eric looked as if he'd scored a point. "Just be a pig, and gulp up anything you can."

"Those are your words, and those are your hang-ups. And you're welcome to them."

"Do you"—Jeremy was embarrassed but made himself go on—"sleep with a lot of girls?"

"Ah no, Jeremy. The sexual revolution is still more talk than action. And I'm still caught in that Puritan quicksand. I mean, if a girl is instantly available then I figure there's something wrong with her, that I'm taking advantage of somebody who's sick. It sounds inconsistent, doesn't it, and I suppose it is, but I can't shake that feeling. Anyway, if I *were* a pig, I'd have no problems about that. No, I have to build up to that, and usually by then I've either seen somebody else I'm much more curious about or the girl gets to where if we did it, it would be like I'm signing a contract, and I don't like contracts."

"You know," Eric said, "it's *you* that's just talk."

"Oh, I get my satisfactions, even if I haven't gone all the way but a few times."

"You warming up for college?" Jeremy asked. "There's more—uh—complete action there from what I've heard."

"Doesn't look as if I'll get to college for a while."

"How come? You've got no problem with grades."

"I'm not going to register for the draft is why."

"What kind of idiocy is that?" Eric scratched his head.

"I don't believe anybody has the right to make me kill. There is no one in this world I want to kill. And nobody can make me. If I register, I'm saying that I recognize that somebody has that kind of power over me. Even if I apply for a C.O. exemption, I'm recognizing their right to give me that exemption. And I don't."

"That's five years, friend, *five years.*" Eric was shaking his head. "You either have a martyr complex or you've freaked out. I wouldn't have believed it until now, but maybe grass does affect the mind."

"What amazes me," Mike said, "is that my position is

so rare. Think about it. Why do you give anybody the right to tell you to kill somebody?"

"Because," said Eric, "of the social contract. You live in a country and it does some things for you, and you have certain responsibilities to it."

"Yes, I have some. But killing isn't one of them. There are some things nobody can make me do to myself. No country, nobody."

"There's one thing you've forgotten," Jeremy said. "If you stay out, if you go to jail, somebody's going to have to take your place."

"I haven't forgotten that. But I don't feel guilty about it. He has the same choice I have. If he goes along with the system, then that's something he'll have to live with."

"What do your parents say?" Jeremy leaned forward, looking at him closely.

"My mother wants me to go to a psychiatrist. My father doesn't believe me. He thinks I'm just talking brave but when the time comes, I'll go for a 2-S."

"And what makes you so sure you won't?" Eric smirked.

"I've never been so sure of anything in my life. It may be the only thing I'm sure about."

Jeremy kept looking at him. He wanted, corny as it was, to shake his hand, to do or say *something* to show Mike how much he admired what he was going to do. And how much he envied him. Whatever that meant. What did it mean? It meant he, Jeremy Wolf, had no balls. Something he'd been suspecting for a long time.

chapter 10

It had been a strange lunch. Hershey had been strange.
No talk about new contracts he'd gotten or new lectures
he'd given on motivational research in graduate seminars
when Hershey didn't even have an M.A. He hadn't
ordered dessert. He'd taken three puffs from his cigar,
and had ground it out. Sam had enjoyed the lunch, as
he was now enjoying one of Hershey's cigars.

"You know what my wife found in Lila's handbag
last night?" Hershey glared at him. How would he

know? Lila was a quiet, homely girl. What could there have been in her handbag?

"Marijuana," Hershey answered his own question, spitting out the word as if he'd just tasted something terribly sour. "An envelope with marijuana in it. Have you any idea what I've contributed to that school's building fund? That exclusive school. That school is so exclusive I suppose it's only the best marijuana."

"She told you she got it in school?"

"First she told us it wasn't marijuana. They were studying different kinds of herbs, can you imagine? I make $70,000 a year, and my own daughter treats me like I go to an astrologer or something. The nerve, the sheer nerve, trying to pull something like that on me. So it came out. Kids in the school are selling it."

"Does the school know?"

"There's a strict rule. Anybody caught with marijuana —out! So what do I do? If I call him up, who will he throw out? Her."

"Well, if you've contributed to the building fund . . ."

"No, it's not that kind of school. They have integrity. They're blind, but they have integrity. Even if they didn't kick her out, it would be a mark against her."

"So what did you do?"

"That girl is grounded for the rest of the year. Home by four o'clock every day. No dates. No nothing outside the house. And if it happens again—"

"Yes?" Sam was always interested in learning of the possibility of new sanctions.

"If it happens again, well, I told her it was so awful a punishment, I wouldn't tell her right away, I'd give her another chance."

"What is it?"

"I don't know, damn it, I haven't thought of anything yet. You got any ideas?"

"No allowance."

"I thought of that. Her mother would slip her something on the side. I tell you there's no trust anymore, not in business, not in a marriage, somebody's always sneaking something."

"You could tell her you'd send her away to boarding school."

"Hah! Just what she'd like. Freedom! She yells, 'Free-Dum!' like she was some native going off to the hills with a gun. Who knows what she'd get into in a boarding school? You think I want a baby in the house, at my age?"

"There are very strict boarding schools."

"None of them are that strict any more. Oh, they've got rules, but these kids—the stricter the rule, the more a challenge it is. No, no boarding school. I want her where I can watch her."

"So what are you going to do?"

"Watch her."

"And the ultimate punishment?"

"Let her imagine. Maybe she has a better imagination than I have. You know, come to think of it, that's the best punishment. Let *them* imagine it. Yeah. Now, I feel better. I've accomplished something."

Hershey took out another cigar. "And *your* boy?"

"Not marijuana yet, not so far as I know. But what do I know? To know what's happening with your kids these days you have to take a course in criminal investigation. And interrogation too. You're the expert on motivation. Why is all this? What the hell do they want?"

"Look, what did we want when we were kids? To do better than our fathers. What did we have? Nothing we didn't get ourselves. That took a lot of energy, a lot of time. There wasn't anything left for this kind of nonsense. We made things too easy for our kids, you know that as well as I do."

"So what's the answer? You can't manufacture the old conditions."

"The answer? Watch them and pray, pray they don't do too much damage to themselves until they're on their own. And then you pray they *will* be on their own. How many men do you know who are still kicking in something every month to a divorced daughter? Or a married daughter. It makes no difference."

"Quite a few."

"Exactly. My father used to be afraid there'd be no one to take care of him in his old age. Maybe that's why he dropped dead when he was fifty. Now it's getting to be the other way around. Can you make enough money until the end so you can support your children and *their* families in the style to which you've accustomed them? We could be trapped, Sam. Trapped for good."

"Not Jeremy. Once he leaves, I'll be surprised to get a postcard a year."

"Hah! Wait. Keep up your health, Sam, you're going to need it."

He's probably right, Sam thought. It's like welfare. You get them used to dependency.

"And then there'll be grandchildren, Sam. Nice, cuddly grandchildren who'll get heavier and heavier."

chapter 11

The way it worked, Mr. O'Connor had explained, each kid they were tutoring would talk into a tape recorder. Talk about himself, about his neighborhood, or make up stories. Anything he wanted to do. Then what he'd said would be transcribed and given back to him in a folder that would be the start of his own book. The idea was that a kid's reading would get better because he'd want to read what he had, in a sense, written himself. And also, in time, his writing would get better because he'd want to keep adding to his book, and there wouldn't always be a tape recorder around when the spirit moved him. That was the theory. But in front of Jeremy was a fourteen-year-old boy, black and stiff and silent.

"Isn't there anything you want to talk about?"

The boy just barely shook his head.

"How about what you want to be when you grow up?"

The boy kept staring at the tape recorder.

Jeremy was sweating outside while panic swelled inside.

"Do you know any jokes?"

The boy shook his head.

Jeremy shut off the machine, ran his hand down his face, and shook his head.

"What would you like to do?"

"Go home."

"Then why did you come here?"

"My mother said she'd give it to me good if I didn't."

"Listen, let's forget the machine. If you could have anything you wanted right now, what would it be?"

"Money. Lots of money. Money's the most beautiful thing. Without it you're nothin'."

"What would you do with it?"

"I'd know what to do with it."

Jeremy was trying frantically to figure out a way to keep the conversation going. The boy looked out the window. Jeremy saw Mr. O'Connor stop at the door. "Excuse me," he said to the boy. The boy kept looking out the window. Jeremy motioned to Mr. O'Connor to follow him into the corridor.

"I can't do anything with him." Jeremy kept his voice as low as he could. "Nothing works."

"O.K., calm down. I'll spend some time with him. Why don't you walk around and see what's happening in some of the other classrooms."

Across the hall he looked through the window in the door and saw Mike with a small, wiry Negro girl of about thirteen. She was jabbering into the machine and Mike was grinning. For one blazing moment, Jeremy hated Mike and the girl and that lump of a boy he'd left behind him. He heard an angry voice down the hall.

"Take your goddamn hat off."

In that room, as he looked in, he saw Criss, a Negro girl a year below him in the school. He'd seen her often in the corridor but he didn't know her. She was thin, but not skinny, and her face—well, if he was an artist, that's the kind of face he'd like to paint. High cheek bones, a firm but perfectly proportioned jaw line, and deep black eyes. She wore her hair natural, they called it, but she kept it closely cropped. Her face was like the rest of her, finely, gracefully made. And he liked the way she stood. Like an arrow. Way back, he fantasied, there was an African princess who'd been stolen and sold, and she comes from her. Criss glanced at him.

"Mind if I watch? I'm just starting."

She shrugged her shoulders, and turned to a tall, broad boy, slouched in his seat, a cap on his head.

"Maurice, do you wear a hat at home?"

"Nope."

"Then get it off. You're such a big man, show some respect."

The boy couldn't have been much younger than she was. With a sheepish grin, he yanked his cap off.

"Now then," she smiled, "have you added anything to your book?"

The boy nodded, turned the pages of his folder, and handed it to Criss. As she read, she shook her head approvingly. "You've really got something going here. They could make this into a movie."

In envy, Jeremy walked on. In the other classroom he looked into there was Eric, and he had something going too. Jeremy trudged back to where he was supposed to be and, standing at the door, he watched as Mr. O'Connor turned on the tape machine. From it came the voice of the boy. "And then a ray came out of his fingers and wham, the whole army was burnt up."

"What was his next adventure?" O'Connor said as he turned on the machine.

"I gotta think about that." Jeremy came into the room, and the boy ignored him. "Hey," he said to O'Connor, "doesn't that thing itch?"

O'Connor touched his beard. "Only at the very beginning. After a while, you forget it's there."

"I'm gonna have one of those," the boy said.

O'Connor looked at his watch. "The bus must be downstairs. See you next time, Joe."

The boy nodded, walked past Jeremy, stopped, said, "I can eat your brain without saying a word," and went out the door.

Jeremy, his mouth open, looked after him. He shivered. "What did *that* mean?"

"Joe has a very vivid imagination, and a lot of anger. A whole lot."

"How did you get him to talk?"

"I asked him what he liked on television, and from there we went into the kind of television show he'd invent."

"This isn't my thing, Mr. O'Connor. I just can't make contact."

"It's only your first time. Give it a try."

"No. I just don't have it."

Criss walked in and handed Mr. O'Connor a folder. "Read this," she said. "I don't know if it's true or not, like he says, but it sure moves." She looked at Jeremy. "How did you do?"

"I didn't. I don't have the knack for this."

"Too bad. You might have learned something."

"Think about it, Jeremy," O'Connor said. "It takes time. On both sides."

"Takes more than time," said Criss. "It takes soul."

"But soul isn't an exclusively black property?" O'Connor said, filling his pipe.

"Mostly. Some of you got some, but most of you don't."

"How can you tell about me so soon?" said Jeremy.

"I didn't make any judgment. I was just telling you what it takes."

"Boy, we really had something going today," Mike came in, and put his arm around Criss. She twisted away.

"Watch yourself, friend," she said coolly. "We've been freed."

"Oh, I know, I know." Mike laughed. "You coming to the meeting tonight?"

"Nope. You know how I feel about that."

"What meeting?" asked Jeremy.

"There's a thing about a demonstration when that general comes to speak next week. You want to come?"

"I don't know if I can get out," said Jeremy.

"Poor boy," Criss shook her head, "you ain't been freed yet."

chapter 12

A heart attack at forty-nine. He looked up from the obituary page and scanned the crowded cafeteria. How many of you have one day left? A month? A year? Paul Stone at forty-nine. He'd hardly thought of him since they had been in high school together. A smart boy, cool, tough, on the inside. Pleasant enough, but remote. Sam knew he'd gone into law, but until just then Sam hadn't realized Paul had become important enough to rate three paragraphs in the *Times*. That's it, Paul.

You've had it. Sam stared into his coffee, and sighed. When would it come to him? And how? A terrible, terrifying pain down his arm, across his chest, and then black? Or something that takes longer, puts you in a hospital bed, knowing that's the last stop? He saw himself looking out the hospital window at people alive in the street. How would he take it? He'd take it. What choice would he have? Truth is truth. He'd make the best of it. What does that mean? He'd hide his fear, that's what it meant, because nobody would really give a damn anyway. Lillian would sit there with her fake cheerfulness, aching to get out of the room. Jeremy would stare at him, and he'd stare at Jeremy. He'd just as soon the kid stayed home. He'd just as soon Lillian stayed home. He felt his eyes water and was disgusted at himself. But what was wrong with a little self-pity?

He got up, paid his check, and went into the street. Ahead of him were two thin girls with long hair. No, one was a boy. Freedom. They want freedom, they take freedom. For what? To have their hair grow long. One thing I know, and you don't, he looked at the boy's back. You're going to be thirty and then forty and then fifty. You can't escape, with your long hair. You think you're going to be different than I am. You're going to *be*, not just exist. Yeah. Wait. Wait until the bills start coming in. You've got pressures now. Everybody's trying to process you, huh? You don't know what pressures are. Take my advice. Slit your throat. That'll be your contribution to society. They'll put your name on a plaque for having helped curb the population explosion.

So this is what hate is. Looking at that boy, he hadn't felt such hate in years. Well, it's better than self-pity. No. He was disgusted with himself again. A hell of a way to start the day. Maybe he should stop reading the obituary page. At least not so early in the morning.

At the reception desk Miss Hamilton smiled like she really meant it. "Good *morning,* Mr. Wolf."

"I'm glad for you," he said, walking by. Now what was the point of that? I bet some girl is smiling this morning at Paul Stone's office. Why not?

"The letter on top," his secretary handed him his mail. "Internal Revenue. They want to examine last year's returns."

"Of course, Vera."

"Oh, you expected it?"

"There's no end to what I expect. That's not quite true. There is an end. Maybe we should be grateful for that."

"I don't quite follow you, Mr. Wolf."

"You will, Vera. You will."

chapter 13

Sitting beside O'Connor's desk was a tall, gnarled white-haired man whose eyes, Jeremy felt, seemed to cut into you. It wasn't that his look was fierce. It was just too direct for comfort. It was like he was trying to get into your head. Jeremy quickly looked down, and when he looked up again, the man was drilling into Tracy. Jeremy hadn't wanted to come because he'd never heard of Frederick Lewis, but Mike had been curious, so he went along.

There were about twenty kids in the room—some from

Jeremy's class, a few juniors, and a couple of sophomores and freshmen. Criss was in the front row, looking almost as cool and hard as Lewis. O'Connor got up, glanced at his watch, and said, "Dr. Lewis is in this country to look into some of our schools. He is, as I'm sure many of you know, a distinguished physicist, but he's also written on poetry and politics, and a particular concern of his in recent years has been education. He wanted to get to know some of you, what your concerns are, and I thought it would be—uh—educational for you to know him. I suppose I should say, to maybe get things started, that we have one fundamental disagreement. I'm a pacifist, and he believes that in certain circumstances violence is not only justified but is essential to achieve just ends."

"I am not, however," Lewis said in a crisp English accent Jeremy envied, "Dr. Strangelove."

"You had a lot to do with the bombing during the Second World War, didn't you?" Mike asked.

"Not a lot in the sense that I was anywhere near in charge. I was part of the staff which designed a number of raids."

"The lives that were lost as a result of those raids, did that bother you?"

"In time of war, that question doesn't really occur to you. Certainly not in that war. My job was to help end that war as quickly as possible, and in any case, the sooner the war did end, the fewer the casualties."

"Afterwards. Were you bothered afterwards?" Mike was leaning forward.

"Let me say, first, that early on in the war, my sister's life was ruined because her husband was killed in London during a German bombing raid. A man, a Jew, who had been a professor of mine in Berlin, was placed in a concentration camp and was never heard of again. I was very fond of that man, and owed him an enormous amount. So personally—and I can give you many other examples—I was convinced that what I was doing was right. After the war, I was indeed bothered, but much more by the millions whom the Nazis had killed, in and out of concentration camps, than by those whose deaths we had been responsible for. You see, I knew pacifists during that war and they remained steadfast and pure, I suppose you would say. We dirtied our hands, but we did end the war."

"To what purpose?" O'Connor turned to him. "From that war came nuclear arms and the very likely possibility that we shall all get blown up, by accident or design, sooner or later. Probably sooner."

"We were not seers," Lewis said drily, "and even if we had been, we were dealing with a maniac who had to be stopped. You can argue *ex post facto*, if you like, that mass nonviolent resistance—among the Jews, among the peoples of the occupied countries—might eventually have stopped Hitler. But there was no such mass nonviolent resistance; you can hardly count Denmark as making any difference. The choice, it seemed to me then, was clear. I have no regrets about having made that choice."

"Not even about Dresden?" said Mike, his face tight.

"You killed 135,000 civilians in Dresden, and that's what you intended to do. There were hardly any military targets there."

"You are assuming, which I did not at the time, that people not carrying guns and not in uniform are innocent. Sometimes they are, and sometimes they are not. The vast majority of the German people supported Hitler and were part of the civilian war machine. Similarly, I was not appalled in principle by the Germans' bombing England. You see, except for the pacifists—standing pure and irrelevant—everyone in a nation at war is a combatant. If you pay your taxes, if you help manufacture uniforms, if you process food, you are *involved*. No man is an island, least of all in war. Except the absolute pacifists. And I do respect them for their consistency. They do none of those things. But no one else is innocent. As in your country. Students who get deferments, professors who march in dissent but file income tax returns, are hardly out of it. I say file, mind you. Holding off a bit of your taxes in some sort of protest game is quite absurd, because the government will take it anyway, with interest besides."

"What about those who resist the draft?" said Mike.

"The selective pacifist, you mean, who will not cooperate in any way. Yes, I would say he has retained his innocence of wrongdoing, as he would put it, in a particular war. He has been willing to pay a price, a high price, for his convictions. He has, if you use those words, saved his own soul, by those standards of soul-saving. But he hasn't stopped the war. That again is the dirty job of the quite impure politicians, military men, and some scientists."

"If you were an American of draft age," O'Connor was tamping down the tobacco in his pipe, "would you participate in the war we're in now?"

Lewis paused before answering, looking at some invisible spot directly in front of him. "If I were a young man of draft age I would have a serious problem, and I can't tell you easily what I would do. It's the kind of hypothetical question anyway that has no force because it has no substance in reality. Let me say this instead and speculate instead that I were who I am but an American. I do think your government is wrong, both politically and—I do use the term occasionally—morally. Therefore, I would have to assess where I could best contribute to ending the war—from inside or in protest from without. From inside by persuasion, which would not work, since scientists are not taken seriously in that area by politicians. And then perhaps by devising some method, violent indeed but non-nuclear, by which the other side's capacity to resist would be shattered so completely that the war would be instantly ended, thereby not involving other powers. If I could not accomplish the latter, I would try to join with others in political opposition from the outside."

"But if you think the war immoral," Criss said, staring at him, "how could you engage in it in any way, for whatever purpose?"

"Because, my dear, my concern is not remaining pure but being relevant. I quite agreed with the American decision to drop the atom bomb on Hiroshima because in the long run, it saved many more lives than it cost. But at that time, no one else had nuclear arms. In this case, since I do not consider the war moral, my concern would be all the more urgent to save lives on both sides. And if a large act of violence would end the war, not spread it, I would participate in it. Tell me, are you opposed to torture?"

"I suppose I'd say yes," said Criss, "but I haven't really thought about it."

"I have." Mike's voice was loud. "And I *am* opposed to it, unconditionally."

"Unconditionally. Indeed. Let us consider the possibility that one man, if successfully tortured, could save many lives. Let me make it as difficult for you as I can. This is a man you are sure has knowledge of a plan to wipe out a village of people, many of them children, in an adjoining country not involved in the war, as a means to get that country into it. In these wars of national liberation, as they call them, this is a realistic possibility. If you tortured the one man, you could save that village and many other people in that country later. Would that be a condition for you?"

Everyone was looking at Mike. "I wouldn't be there to take part in that decision. I'd be in jail for having resisted the draft."

"You would, in sum, be pure."

"Yes, and hoping that by my example, and the example of others, there would eventually be enough people who are pure, as you put it, so that we could never even get into a war again."

"Granted the achievement of your utopian hope, then

your own country would be pure. But what of the people in that village?"

"If we weren't there," said Mike, "there would be no need for the nationalists to engage in violence."

"But what if some other country *were* there in opposition to them?"

"My answer is the same, only as applied to nations. This country, by example, would show the way to others."

"And if, having gone to jail and thereby having retained your innocence, in this narrow sense of the word, you saw by the time you were sixty or seventy that your country had not changed and the world had not changed?"

Mike stood up and jammed his shaking hands into his pockets. "Look, there are some things you have to do whether they work or not, whether you know that they're going to work or not. Violence is *wrong!* War is *wrong!* Maybe it wasn't against the Nazis. I don't know. I wasn't around then. But I do know it's wrong now and I'm not going to be part of it. You killed a lot of people, and that doesn't seem to have bothered you very much. I don't want to be like that. And if I let you trap me by what you call reason and logic, I could become like that. I'm just not going to be part of it. Maybe that's being irrelevant, but you've got to start somewhere if you want to change the world, and I'm starting with myself."

He sat down again, his hands still in his pockets.

There was silence until O'Connor, a cloud of smoke coming from his pipe, said to Lewis, "Checkmate?"

Lewis smiled. "We shall see. I would certainly like to lose this game, and there is a possibility that man will eventually get to the point at which war will appear wholly ludicrous to him. And perhaps people like this young man may accelerate the coming of that time. But I see a quite different likelihood."

"Which is?" O'Connor took the pipe out of his mouth.

"We have never had weapons which were not eventually used. People talk of the horror of a nuclear war, but except for a relatively few Japanese, who have been largely forgotten, they do not know that horror in any sense that they can *feel*. I think peace may come only through the experience of that kind of horror. And even then I'm not sure. It is a cliché to say that the war after the nuclear war will be fought with clubs and stones. But you will notice they say it *will* be fought. Still, we will not be going back to the beginning of history in all respects, and that gives me a certain amount of hope that all of it will not be repeated."

"But right now *we're* history," Mike said.

"Yes." Lewis barely smiled. "So we are. I shall take your name down, young man, and shall hope to hear it again."

chapter 14

"Is that all you know about your father?"

"Use your fork. I take it you don't have a principled objection to using a fork instead of your fingers."

"But that's weird. You were over thirty when he died. How come you never asked him more about himself?"

Irritated, Sam looked at his son, again taking a piece of steak with his fingers. How come, how come? Did you ever ask me anything about myself? About where I lived when I was a kid? About what I wanted to be? "Because," he said, "there always seemed to be enough time left to ask, when I was interested enough to really pursue it. In the meantime his brother died, and God knows where the cousins went to."

"But what kind of farm was it? I thought Jews weren't allowed to own land in Russia."

"There were exceptions. It had come down from his grandfather. I don't know what kind of a farm. All I remember is he once talked about how he used to like to fish. I suppose it was a farm farm. They raised animals and some kind of grain."

"And you don't know anything about what the life was like, what kind of school he went to, what his parents were like?"

"He had an uncle, some kind of radical. He was arrested in 1905. I don't know what happened to him."

"You didn't even find out more about THAT? With somebody like that in the family, how could you NOT want to know more?"

"Look, I regret it more than you do. While there was time, I didn't think it was that important. Now it's as if I came out of a void. We start here, Jeremy."

"It *is* kind of creepy, being able to go only so far back. But good too. There's no weight of ancestors, of traditions."

"It's not always a burden, I think, that kind of weight. I used to go with a girl who could trace her family all the way back to England in the sixteenth century. I envied her, and I suppose I had a kind of awe of her just because of that. Why the sudden curiosity?"

"Criss, she's a girl in school, was going on about she was part Indian four generations back, and on the other side, she says, were freedmen, starting in 1800 or something. So I began wondering who there'd been in back of me."

"That reminds me. I did find out something about my great-grandfather, the one who bought the land. My father said he remembered him, a big man with a long white beard, riding a big horse and carrying a gun."

"Wow! A Jew with a gun in Russia!"

"That *was* rare."

"It must have made you feel good."

"Until I started thinking about it. What kind of a Jew would have been allowed to carry a gun in those days? An Uncle Tom. Maybe you're right. Maybe it's better not to go back too far."

"Well, I'm going to have trouble explaining some things to *my* kids."

"Like what?"

"Like my father was part of a magazine that took ads, that went after ads, from a company that made napalm. I was looking through it last night. I almost threw up."

"Oh, for Christ's sake. You want to be logical, you want to be pure, some part of my commission from those ads went into what you're eating, into your clothes, into your goddamned hi-fi set. Grow up. You and your moral judgments. You've got two choices. You go into a monastery or you become part of the world. You become part of the world, you become part of all of it—the good, the bad, the lying, the cheating, the exposing, the covering up again. Once you make that choice, the rest is a matter of degree. You try to stay as straight as you can, and part of that is getting rid of any illusions you haven't been bent a little and won't be bent again."

"But you do the bending to yourself. You're putting it in the passive sense."

"Very smart. Simplistic, but smart. Shallow smart. You won't believe anything I tell you anyway so I'll let you win that point. But you ought to get your priorities straight. That company hasn't broken any law. That company has done what its government asked it to do. What kind of moral faker would I be if I said 'No, that company is too dirty to be in our magazine'? What would that win me? Where else would I draw the line? Every company that advertises with us has some kind of government contract, some of them secret. If I start drawing any kind of line, I go out of business."

"Maybe that would be a good idea, since you're in that kind of business."

"Brilliant. Just brilliant. From where you are, it's all so easy. Boy, I hope to live long enough to see you when you're my age."

"Yes, sir, there it is, an authentic American father's curse. God, what a crummy country."

"You know better ones?"

"Sure. Cuba, Sweden, just to start."

"I'll give you another wish. That you live long enough in either one of them to learn that basically it's no different there either."

"For you it wouldn't be. You've been bent too far."

Sam got up. "Listen, holy man, what kind of choices have you ever had to make? Which color sport shirt?

Which show on television? You come judge me when you know what it's all about. In the meantime enjoy your corrupted food."

"I'm thinking about a choice. I'm thinking about not registering for the draft."

"You are out of your goddamn mind!"

"That's what I thought you'd say. Do you suppose your great-grandfather, when Jews tried to get out of going into the army, would ride after them and catch them?"

Sam looked down at him, and shook his head. "Somebody put a curse on me. And it's going to get worse. Listen, don't say anything to your mother until you really do come to that decision. It'll kill her."

"No, it won't. She'll make noises like it's killing her, but she'll survive."

Sam slapped the boy's face hard. "Just a little concern, you little bastard," he said through his teeth, "just a little concern for somebody else."

Jeremy rose, steadied himself against the table. "I'm talking about something very important to me, and you act like I'm a nuisance. I don't know if I'm going to do it, I don't think I have the courage to do it, but talk about concern, Jesus, the only concern you have is to keep things running smoothly. Nice and orderly. The way you figure it, you've paid my way out of the draft, so why aren't I grateful or at least smart enough not to make waves? It would never occur to you that this is a decision *I* have to make, would it? WOULD IT?"

Sam stared at him. "All right. It's your life, go ahead and make a mess of it."

chapter 15

"You're not serious?" Tracy looked at him as if he'd changed shape during the night—grown another ear or something.

"I don't know if I'm serious or not. Right now I guess I'm not, but I want to be. At least I think I want to be." Jeremy wished he could have come on like lightning. Shazam! Firm of eye, back straight in resistance, a non-violent Che Guevara. The moral force, the courage radiating from him would short circuit that overblown guitarist, and the new Jeremy would draw her, rushing to be filled with his light, into his arms. But actually he felt a little nauseated. There was a lump of fear, for one thing, fear that he might be serious. I mean, he thought, it would be just me against the whole goddamn government.

Eric, amused, bit into a slice of pizza. "Of course, he's not serious. What's the point of going to jail when you can walk right into college for four years? You want to protest? What kind of protesting can you do in jail? Whom are you going to convert? The guards? The whole thing is silly, just plain silly. All right, Mike is something else. He's practically a whole different species. I don't understand him, except that he's going to be one of those professional agitators. Hell, he needs jail time on his record to be a success. But Jeremy, here, Jeremy's one of us. Being a martyr isn't his bag."

Peter, head against the wall, eyes half-closed, broke off his humming, and laughed. "You don't know. I never quite figured this one. There may be depths there beyond our ability to understand. Sitting among us all these years may have been the Sir Thomas More of our time. Can you stand up to the king, Sir Jeremy, even if it means your head? You'd better get a haircut, it'll be quicker and cleaner that way."

"Cut it out." Tracy glared at Peter. She's mad for me, Jeremy watched her. Well, she's mad on my account, that's something.

"Say yes to the boys who say no," Peter was grinning. "You going to do your part, Lady Tracy?"

Jeremy's cheeks were hot, and although he tried to be

angry at Peter, he was glad he'd said it. If I do, *will* you do your part, Tracy?

"You reduce everything to basic irrelevancies," Tracy turned on Peter. "That's a real gift you have."

It's not irrelevant, Jeremy was shouting inside. I mean, it is, connecting sex with the draft, but you're not irrelevant to me, your saying yes couldn't be more relevant to me.

"I'm late." Tracy stood up.

"I'll walk you to the subway," Jeremy said.

"Aha!" Eric waved his fork. "There *is* a method to his madness. Better wait, Tracy. Make him deliver before you do."

"You're disgusting, both of you." Tracy led the way. Outside, they walked in silence for a while. "I guess this isn't the best time to ask," Jeremy spoke in the direction of his feet, "but would you like to go to a movie Friday night?"

"Can't this week. Maybe next though."

They were at the subway stop. "Don't rush into anything." She stood on her toes, pecked at his cheek and was already down the steps before his hands knew what was happening. "If you're going to be serious," she called back, "be serious."

Now what did that mean? He watched her until she was out of sight. Nothing, that's what it meant. A friend she was, just a friend. A concerned friend. Damn. There weren't going to be any rewards for this one, if he did it. Except that he'd finally have done something clear and right. No question it was right. You register, and that makes you part of it. He'd seen it, he'd looked it up in the library. *A Fact Paper on Selective Service.* He pulled his notebook out of his pocket, and read it again: "The law places upon every registrant the liability and responsibility to register, to provide his local board with adequate evidence to permit a judgment 'in the national interest' (not the registrant's interest), and to serve in the Armed Forces if found to be 'available.' " (Please, sirs, can't you find it in the national interest not to make me a killer? Don't be ridiculous, young man, do you want them Communists swarming up the street, raping your sister? I don't have a sister. Your girl friend, then? But that's not the point, sirs, they're not attacking this country. Young man, we can't take the time to argue with every Tom, Dick and Jeremy. You've got to have confidence that your President, on the basis of all the information, and only *he* knows all the information, has made the right decision in the national interest. You just sign up, and in four years, after you get out of college, we'll see where you fit in best. I'll think about it, sirs. Ain't nothing to think about. You've got seven months and three days. You all come in and register or we all are going to come and get you. See, ain't nothing to think about. You got no choice, boy. Yes, I do, I don't have to register at all. Symbolic action, boy, that's all it is, symbolic action. Waste of time. Face up, face up. Be a man! But I don't choose to be that kind of man. Hear that, Joe? He doesn't *choose* to be that kind of man. Well, with that hair, I can see where he has a problem. But that'll be all fixed up. Son, the Army's the best thing that could happen to you. If I was your father, I'd say you ought to go right straight in, and go to college after. You'll get a lot more out of that higher schooling, being a man. Sirs, I think you're crazy. I think the whole country's crazy. Boy, what qualifications you got to make that kind of judgment? Trouble with you is, you don't appreciate being an American. You've had it too soft, boy. That's the trouble with kids like you. But sirs, why do I have to kill? For peace, damn it! Can't you see that? How can we have peace if we don't stop those people who are always aggressing against it? But aren't we aggressing, sirs? Boy, I tell you, education has just gone to hell. Don't you know the difference between aggressing and defending freedom?)

"Hey." Criss poked his shoulder. "Wake up. How come you weren't at the tutorial? Have you really dropped out?"

"Yeah. I'm no good at it. Like I said, I just don't have whatever that takes."

"And you're the one who's going to defy the United States Government?"

"You heard?"

"Sure I heard. I just saw pothead Peter. Well, I'll believe it when I see it, and then I'll look again."

"And if I do go through with it, will that excuse me from dropping out?"

"One has nothing to do with the other. Besides, I don't care what you do, any of you, one way or the other."

"Not even Mike? Or O'Connor?"

"They're the same color as you. If you can call it a color. All washed out, it looks to me."

"You mean there's no difference between any of us?"

"I didn't say that. You all have very low priority with me, that's all. Very low. Some of you I like better than others, but I don't really give a damn about any of you."

"Well, I can understand that, I suppose."

"No, you can't."

She walked away. Jeremy, shoving his hands deeper into his pockets, leaned against a building and imagined himself holding Tracy very hard. But she wasn't looking at him. She was looking over his shoulder at something.

chapter 16

Jack's coming to dinner. Not with the female hippo-
potamus? The message just said Jack. No answer at
home. For once he and the boy would be on the same
side. That's what this family needed. A common enemy.
A boarder. We should find a boarder the three of us
detest. Think of the intimate sharings of space and gossip
when he wasn't there. The winks behind his back. The
delight at his bad news. Obnoxious boarders could shore
up the weakening middle-class family. The marriages

that would be saved! The generation gap sealed against the outsider.

In the office across the street there was a girl he hadn't seen before. Trim. Very trim. A figure like Mary's. Mary then. Probably Mary now too. She'd already had two children then, and she still had the figure of a girl. I could have talked her into a divorce, but who needed somebody else's children? But if I had, we'd have had our own too. She'd be almost fifty now. All right, she is almost fifty now, but as removed from me as if she were dead. Somebody to talk to. What would it be like to come home to somebody you wanted to talk to?

Again. Again you're slipping into self-pity. Enough. What is, is. You don't have cancer, so far as you know. You don't have heart trouble, so far as you know. Your backhand has gotten much better. But what about sex? Not the wham-bam-thank-you-ma'am at home, but something to look forward to? Kay, Lishinsky's secretary. Yes, long, long legs, long red hair. Watching her move along the hall is an aesthetic experience, sex aside. But absolutely nobody ever on the office staff. The one place he functioned well, the one place he was in control, had to be kept secure. It would be unendurable, mixing business and conspiracy, even if it was for pleasure. He'd fall apart, and one thing Sam Wolf is never going to do is fall apart. A call girl? He'd feel a fool, he'd be a fool. A man who has to pay for it has no self-respect. The thing to do is get up another tennis game for a second night a week. He'd feel better all around.

88

Was the kid serious? Not likely. Talk. *Épater le papa.*
I'm going to ignore it. It's his move. If I say something,
he may make a move he doesn't want to make. Let the
natural juices of self-protection do their work. If he had
taken Mary, there would have been no Jeremy. Impossible to really imagine, of course, but anyway, aside from
the fact that you have to love your own child, there was
something there he also liked. As irritating as the kid
was, there was a stubbornness he kind of admired. When
the kid wasn't there, he admired it. It could be that after
the kid left home, they'd have a better relationship. That
was something to look forward to. You see, if you take
the time to list your assets and possibilities, there's no
call for self-pity.

Going out the door, he saw Kay waiting for the eleva-
tor, and sighed. Inconspicuously. There was time, he had
just enough time to get a new racket. A steel one. Makes
your game crisper, faster. Anyway, that girl would be no
one to talk to. All he ever saw her carry were *Vogue*
and *Harper's Bazaar.* You got through, you'd look at
each other, and what would you talk about? The office?
You're a wise man, Sam Wolf, to keep things in order.
The pleasures of order are not to be underestimated. His
desk was clean. Each pen was in the right place in his
pockets. He would be home at exactly 6:45, as always.
She smiled at him, a perfectly appropriate, professional,
end-of-the-day smile. What if, he wondered in the ele-
vator, she suddenly took his hand? Thank God, he didn't
have to worry about things like that. He was past the age

of believing in the unexpected—of *that* nature. Well past. And that was a relief. A small sadness, but essentially a relief.

She went right, he went left. As it should be. Well, that was his adventure for the day. An adventure without risk. The best kind. If he ever got to Sacramento, would he look up Mary, just to see what she looked like now? Sure, why not. But what would ever bring him to Sacramento? Fortunately, nothing.

chapter 17

What the hell was going on in front of the school? One of the little ones, she must be in the fifth grade, was crying, and pointing to a Negro boy of about twelve. He was shaking his head, No, and three other black kids, also not from the school—he could see that, they were so damn hostile—were jumping up and down.

"We don't know nothin' about her bus pass!"

"She lose her bus pass and blame it on us!"

"All we doing is going home!"

O'Connor, shaking his own head, was standing between the girl and the indignant four. Another teacher, Harkness, a Negro, came out the door and moved quickly into the confrontation.

"She's sure this was the one?" he asked O'Connor. The little girl, still pointing, wailed to confirm.

"She outta her mind. I don't need her stinking bus pass."

"Hey, Willie, what're you doing around here?" Criss had whizzed across the street and now stood, her arm around the accused. "My little brother," she smiled at O'Connor and Harkness. The boy gave a quick, sharp glance upward, grinned, and leaned against Criss who gently moved him aside, went over to the crying girl, bent down, and said softly, "You must have been mistaken. You don't really think my little brother would have stolen anything?"

The little girl, bewildered, looked at the smiling boy, at Criss, at O'Connor and Harkness, and stammered between sobs, "But I know it was him."

"Was he in front of you when your pass was taken?"

"No, he came running behind, he grabbed it out of my hand."

"Then you can't be absolutely sure *this* was the boy."

"He was the closest."

"Wait a minute," said O'Connor. "Where's the pass?" There was no pass. Did he eat it? Jeremy wondered, looking around on the ground. Unless it's in one of their pockets, but they're too smart for that.

"Are you *absolutely* sure?" Criss was still kneeling, her face close to the girl's.

"Well, it was *one* of them."

O'Connor scratched his head. The boys, sensing that somebody had to act right now, began to move away, weaving, kind of dancing. " 'Bye, sis," said the formerly accused. "Wait," O'Connor said, but, still seeming to amble, they'd quickened their pace, and then, laughing, disappeared around the corner.

"Here," said Harkness, giving the little girl a dollar. "You'll need another bus pass." O'Connor, eyebrows up, looked at him. Harkness was staring at Criss. "I'd like to see you, young lady, at three o'clock."

"Why, sure, Mr. Harkness. 'Bye all."

"Hey," Jeremy hurried after her, and then found himself whispering, "that wasn't your brother."

Criss, without slowing down, said, "What business is it of yours?"

"None, I suppose, but do you think that was the right thing to do, encouraging a kid to steal?"

"All that's been stolen from that boy, he could take a truckload of stuff from whites every day, and you people would still be owing him."

"But, I mean, how is this going to help *him?* He'll do it again and he'll get caught, he'll get caught too many times and he'll be sent away someplace."

"Maybe he'll get caught and maybe he won't. One thing at a time. He learned something today. He learned that blackness could be a good thing. He knew I saved him because we're both black. That's a very important thing for him to know."

"Criss, suppose you saw a black man mugging somebody, some old white lady?"

"Why not some young white lady? Look, I don't have to deal with your hypothetical situations. I got enough real things on my mind. You think I want that kid to be nothing but a thief? Why the hell do you think I'm in this school? So I can learn where the children of white power learn, learn what they know, and then go back to kids like that and use it against you."

"But we're not like our parents. You won't have to use power against *us!*"

"Hah! I'll believe *that* when I see it."

"Criss," he was finding it hard to swallow and his head hurt, "I don't have anything against anybody. I don't even have any power, and if I had, I'd be glad to share it."

"Good for you. That's a *good* boy." She patted him on the cheek, and walked into the school. Stupid, stupid, stupid. How stupid he must have sounded. Damn, damn, damn. He wished he had a dog so he could kick it and then know exactly why he was feeling guilty.

Behind him he heard O'Connor. "What're you going to say to her?"

"I want to know what she has to say to me, what she thinks she's accomplished," Harkness answered.

"That's easy," O'Connor laughed. "There's one black kid free."

"No, I want to know how carefully she's thought

through where she's going, what it is she wants to do."

"Very carefully, I expect. That Criss is going to be a black national resource."

"If she doesn't corrode herself with hate. Power is one thing, hate is another. And hate can destroy power, your own power."

Harkness passed Jeremy and went into the building. "Was it right what she did?" Jeremy turned to O'Connor.

"If I were Criss," said O'Connor, "I would have probably done the same thing. That's the only clear answer I can give you. And that's not clear at all. We're coming into hard times, Jeremy. There's going to be a terrible weight on each person to know what the right thing is to do. I hear you're feeling some of that."

"I don't know. I say it, but I don't know if I mean it. What did you do in the last war?"

"I was 4F, a heart murmur. That's no help to you."

"What would you do in this one?"

"Jeremy, I can tell you that I would refuse to be drafted, but it's unreal. I'm in no danger of being drafted. Besides, you've really got to come to this decision on your own. I can tell you where to go for advice about the draft, but I expect you know that anyway. What brought you this far? Why are you considering not even registering?"

"If you're drafted, you become part of the killing, right? Or you could be. But even by registering, you say they have the power over you to make you kill or make you go to jail. I mean, if I registered and then applied to be a C.O., and they refused, that would be where it was. And they would refuse. I don't believe in God. I have no past history in any peace church or that kind of thing. But even if I had, even if I were sure they'd let me be a C.O., I'd be giving them that power."

"But you'll go to jail anyway if you don't register."

"Yes, but I wouldn't have given them the power. They'd take it, to put me in jail, but I wouldn't have given it to them."

"I think I hear the words of Mike."

"Yes, he put it in my head, but like you say, I'm the only one who can make the decision. And I don't think I have the courage. I don't think I have anywhere near the courage."

O'Connor looked up from filling his pipe. "I don't know what to say to you, Jeremy. If it means anything, I admire your being able to get yourself into this kind of situation, inside yourself. That takes courage."

"Not really, not yet. God, I wish I was 4F. No offense."

"But you'd still have to register."

"Yeah, I forgot. They really have you boxed in, don't they?"

"Some much more than others. I have a class. Good luck, Jeremy."

"Thanks, but I guess luck isn't part of this, is it?"

chapter 18

"See," Lillian said, "like a clock."

"Right on the button, Sam." Jack raised his glass. "You're an organized man."

I also take a shower every day, Sam thought, do I get another star for that? "Where's the boy?"

"He left half an hour ago. Said there was a very important meeting at the school, some kind of new club he's in."

"Sounds phony to me," Jack laughed. "They're tricky, these young ones."

Takes one to know one. Why doesn't he sit in the

center of the couch? He'll get it all out of shape. Why so solemn all of a sudden? He's looking at me as if he just got a tip on the day of my death.

"Lillian told me something, something very serious." Jack leaned forward.

Her hands were going again, there was fear in her eyes, animal fear. "Jeremy," she said, "Jeremy is thinking of not registering for the draft."

"How do you know?" Did that dumb kid tell her? "He was on the phone this afternoon. I was listening, on the extension, and Eric was trying to argue him out of it. Sam, what are we going to do?"

"You didn't say anything to him about it?"

"I wanted to talk to you first. I'm afraid. You know him, how stubborn he is. You give him the wrong kind of push, and he'll go exactly where you don't want him to. He's always been like that," she said to Jack. "You remember what we used to call him when he was a baby? No-No. Everything was no. Now it's not so cute." The tears were starting. She's going to be a big help.

"You've got to stop him," Jack was rumbling. "You know that. This could kill his career. A murderer can be rehabilitated, but who would hire a draft-dodger? You've got to knock some sense into that kid."

Sam poured himself a drink, a big drink. It was really unfair, that this should have to be on his mind. I do everything by the book. I work hard, I don't take advantage of anybody, I pay all my bills the first of the month. And now this. Isn't it enough that I have to die? Do I have to be Job too?

"Like Lillian says," he sat down opposite Jack, "you don't *knock* anything into this kid. I'm trusting in his good sense. He's never done anything wild, anything self-destructive. I think this will pass. It's something he got out of the air. The air in that school"—he looked at Lillian—"is full of strange things. But I can't believe the kid is going to destroy himself."

"You're not going to do *anything?*" Jack had the look of a cop. A top cop.

"I'm going to talk to him, make sure he understands the full consequences of what he has in mind. What else can I do? Drag him down there and force him to sign up?"

Jack went on, Lillian went on, Sam tuned down the volume, grunting here and there, mumbling something here and there so that he wouldn't be rude, but really out of it. What can I do? No allowance if you don't register. No dates if you don't register. Bread and water if you don't register. What power do I have over the boy in something like this? The power of example? He thinks I'm a sellout. The power of trust in my better judgment, my mature judgment? He thinks I don't know anything that counts. He could walk himself into a jail, and there isn't a damn thing I can do about it.

And there he was. No hat. Of course not. Three degrees outside. Why should he have a hat? No gloves. Must have lost another pair. This is the force that's going to change society. Jeremy, Jeremy, stop rebelling for a minute. Stop and think. Save yourself. That's the first responsibility of any man. Save yourself. But he's not a man. He's been so protected, what does he know about saving himself? But he's not going to do that thing, he can't do it. It'll pass. If I can keep cool, if Lillian can hold down the hysteria, it'll pass.

"Young man," Jack shifted those enormous hams, "that's a very, very stupid thing you're thinking of doing."

"I heard you on the phone," Lillian put her hand out, "with Eric."

The boy hunched his shoulders, he got narrower. God, how thin he is. He hadn't realized how fragile the kid is. You could break him in two like a stick.

"Look," Jeremy took a deep breath, "look, I don't want to talk about it now. I'm not feeling well. Maybe I'm coming down with something. I'm sick to my stomach. I just want to get into bed."

"O.K.," said Sam. "Go ahead. Take some Pepto-Bismol."

"They won't be so kind to you in jail, boy." Jack was a cop again. Or a general. "Think about that, boy. Think about five years in one lousy, stinking, cold cell."

That did it. Lillian's hands were over her face, her back heaving, and those godawful sounds coming out of her.

"Oh Jesus," said Jeremy.

"That's all you have to say?" Jack roared. " 'Oh Jesus?' You're destroying your mother, and all you have to say is 'Oh Jesus'! What are you? What kind of cold fish are you? Did she beat you? Did she starve you? 'Oh Jesus,' he says. I tell you something, I'm glad I don't have any children."

"All right, *enough*, Jack," Sam looked at the floor. "This is no time for any rational discussion." He went over to Lillian, put his hand on her head. "Go to bed, boy. Go to bed. Unless there's something you can tell your mother now."

"I can't be blackmailed out of this!" Jeremy was shouting, his hands still stiff with cold. Look at him. He's taking a stand. He doesn't know enough to wear a hat, and he's taking a stand.

"Blackmail!" Jack lifted himself to his feet, and shook a fat finger at Jeremy. "You're a stupid, ungrateful, self indulgent weakling. You don't have the balls to fight for your country. That's what this is all about. You're scared stiff. Principle! Conscience! You're a coward, that's what you are."

"I said *enough!*" Sam yelled. "You don't know a damn thing about this or about him. You think he's wrong? You think he should put himself in a position where he could get sent to be killed? For what? Who's invading us? If that stupid little country disappeared from the face of the earth, what difference would it make to America? It's a ridiculous war, an insane war!" He stopped. What the hell was this? Jeremy, his mouth open, was looking at him as if he'd turned into somebody else, as if he'd turned into Norman Thomas. Well, he hadn't. "However," he stopped for a second to get his voice down, "you are wrong, boy. Not morally, not on principle. But you're wrong in thinking that what you do will have any effect. It won't. It can't. Not here. Not anywhere. Think, boy. Ten years from now you'll have the satisfaction, maybe, of believing you did the right thing, but if you've ruined the rest of your life in the process, is it worth it? If your going in doesn't change one damn thing, and it won't, is it worth it?"

"You've lost your mind too." Jack's face was red, too red. The guy's going to pop off right there. That'll cap the evening, all right. "No wonder your son is so twisted. What would become of this country if everybody picked out what war he'd fight in and what war he wouldn't?"

"Oh shut up." Sam watched Lillian, moaning now. Yes, sir, a big help she's going to be. "This is my son and this is my problem."

"No," said Jeremy, "it's all mine."

"That's something else you don't know about," Sam poured himself another drink.

chapter 19

He had never been in a courtroom before. Was the building so massive, the ceiling here so high so that everyone in the room would feel small? It was like Justice, huge but invisible, was looking down, keeping a clear, unblinking eye on the judge and the lawyers and the defendants and those who were just watching. Jeremy slid down in his seat.

"I feel kinda left out," Mike said. "They were snatching people from all around me but somehow they never grabbed me."

"I still don't understand the point of it. The General never saw you guys. He went in by some secret entrance and left the same way."

"But that's it, don't you see? It gets in the papers that a four-star general has to sneak into a dinner, and people start to think: How come all those people are out there opposing him? How come he's afraid to face them?"

"Maybe. But what I think they think is: Crack those nuts and sweep what's left off the street."

"Well, the cops think that. Jeez, I don't deny some of the kids were provoking them, but wow, once cops start swinging, they freak out. You should have seen their faces! Man, they HATED us. They didn't even know us, but they hated us. In my whole life nobody's ever looked at me like that. It was scary. I mean I've read stuff about police mentality and how it's a dangerous job so they're uptight all the time and all that, but wow, they're a menace to public order. I'm not kidding. You should have been there. I'll never look at a cop again without flinching inside."

"This guy you know, has he been busted before?"

"No, this was only his third demonstration. He's kind of shaky about this scene. That's why I came down. I mean I would have come down anyway, but I wanted him to see as many friendly faces as possible."

Jeremy had come just out of curiosity. No, it was more than that. He wanted to get a feel of what it was like, courtrooms and judges. In case, you know. In case.

"Synchronize watches. Zorro will be here at 11:02 and spring us all."

Jeremy looked around and saw a red-headed, wiry kid, not a kid, he must have been nineteen. He was grinning at Mike.

"Jeremy, Dan. Dan, Jeremy. How you feel?"

"I'm really dragged but nothing gets me down."

Dan and Mike laughed. "It's a song," Mike said. "It's the first line of a song. We never got any further."

"I don't figure it's going to be bad," said Dan. "Yesterday the guys got suspended sentences if it was their first bust. Of course, that was a different judge."

"All rise," a man in uniform bellowed. In black robes, the judge, small, stocky, his face shut, walked in. "Oh boy," said Dan.

"You can't tell," Mike whispered. "Maybe that's just the way he thinks a judge is supposed to look."

The first case was quick. A tall, thin guy with glasses stood before the judge. He said he was guilty.

"First offense," the judge looked at a piece of paper. "You going to behave from now on? No more of this nonsense, carrying on in the street like a jackass?"

The defendant mumbled something.

"Speak up, speak up! You're big and brave out there in a mob, speak up!"

"No, your honor, I don't plan to demonstrate again for the time being."

"What do you mean, for the time being? Are you going to behave or not?"

There was another mumble. The judge glared down, and Jeremy could barely hear, "Yes, your honor. I will behave."

"Five days. Suspended."

Dan was next. He said he was guilty.

"First offense. Are you going to behave from now on?"

Dan shuffled his feet, and his voice cracked as he started to speak. "Your honor, I don't think I was misbehaving. I considered it my responsibility to protest the war."

"Responsibility? RESPONSIBILITY? You wouldn't know responsibility if you fell on it. Listen, I've got no time to argue with you. You failed to move when instructed by the police. You were disturbing the peace. I will ask you one more time. Are you going to behave yourself?"

There was silence. Dan had gone stiff. He looked up at the ceiling and then at the judge. "Your honor, I don't think you have a right to take into consideration what I may or may not do in the future."

"You're an expert on the war, and now you're an expert on being a judge. Five days. Next."

Jeremy gagged. Oh Jesus, he couldn't throw up in a courtroom. He kept it down. Outside, Mike bought a hot dog and Jeremy avoided watching him eat it.

"You act as if nothing happened," Jeremy said as they walked to the subway.

"It's only five days. I'm just sorry it wasn't me. I really have to get some jail time." Mike stopped and laughed. "What am I going to tell my kids? Daddy fought the good fight and never got busted? Impossible. Oh well, it'll come. Let's see—I'm really dragged but nothing gets me down/ The sky's falling but I got a room underground."

"You can't rhyme down and ground."

"Who says?"

"Mike, what about five years, not five days?"

"Isn't that funny? I forgot for a second that was coming. I guess it's not real until you do it."

"Yeah." Jeremy had to hold it down again.

chapter 20

"No calls, Vera, I have to finish these contracts."

He closed the door. Across the street that girl wasn't there. He sat down and couldn't read. At my age, crying. in the middle of the afternoon. He got up, locked the door, went back to his desk, put his head on his arms, and after a time of darkness, the crying stopped. But he stayed as he was, and in the darkness, he was very small, chubby, stubborn.

"Sam, eat the soup. There are millions of hungry children around the world who would love that soup."

"Give it to them. Let me give it to them. I wish they could have it."

"Sam, don't talk foolish. I'm making a point."

That's right, Mama, I couldn't give them the soup. In *Life*, there was a baby, his stomach bloated, dying of hunger. And I couldn't give him the soup.

"How can I help them, Mama?"

"You grow up to be big and strong and you'll find a way to help them."

That's right, Mama, I pay my taxes, Mama. I pay for grain to India. Why don't I feel good about it, Mama? Why doesn't it mean anything to me?

He raised his head, saw the contracts, and rested his head on his arms again.

Was it so terrible? The boy would serve his time, and he'd still be alive. And maybe this country is changing, maybe by then he'll be, not a hero, but at least a man honored for what he did. By some. By someone who would give him a job in what he wanted to do. It *is* terrible, no way out of that.

"But couldn't you take the money and not buy the soup next time and send them the money?"

"So one child would get one dish of soup. And what would he do the next day?"

"We could keep sending him."

"So one child would have a dish of soup every day, and what of the other children, the millions of them?"

"It's very sad, Mama."

"Yes, it is, Sam. Eat the soup."

He was crying again, for the hungry children, for Jeremy, for himself. What did it matter? It must be past four. I've got to get those contracts in the mail. God, they'd have had to be awfully damn hungry to have liked that soup.

chapter 21

So that's what Robbie looked like, a goddamned sheep dog. His arm was around Tracy. She looked in and waved. Jeremy didn't wave back. O.K., if you take a dumb guitar player over an authentic martyr, then that shows where you are. Damn it. He got up.

"You just sat down." Eric looked at him, frowning.

"Decided I wasn't hungry."

It was mild, a good day for settling it. You could walk through the weather and focus on what had to be done. Or not done. It had to be now, one way or the other. He didn't want to wait so long that his mind would still not be made up with only a week or two to go. If he did decide to do it now, then he'd have time to build his defenses. Against his parents, against himself.

O.K. Easy way. 2S. Four years, maybe more. War would be over then, would have to be. Next war? Worry about that then. Less easy way, but not hard either. Become part of a Quaker meeting or something like that. Register and apply for C.O. They'd see through that. But it *was* real, he didn't want to kill. And with the right counseling, maybe he could make it. After all, this wasn't Iowa or Georgia. Right way. Clear way. I will not be part of their machinery. To what point though? So I'm locked away and then let out, and I won't have changed a thing. I'll have changed myself. How sure can you be of that? You could come out so scared of ever having to go back in again that you'd never take another chance all your life. On anything. How the hell did I get into this? Girls are sure lucky.

He walked and walked, and it still went down the same way. He'd get to the edge of each of the ways and he couldn't make the jump. In a park, he sat down and watched some kids play ball. The sun on him, he stretched out his legs and closed his eyes. I'm really dragged but nothing gets me down. Nothing gets me up either. The sun felt good, so good he stopped thinking.

When he woke it was chilly. And late. But enough time to get home. The kids were gone, the park was still. Why *not* take the easy way? What made him think he was so special? Hell, Thoreau only spent a night in jail, and look at the influence he had. He'd go in for all those years and wouldn't have any influence at all. He was getting mixed up. Would he do it to influence others or because it was something he had to do? What do you mean, *had* to do?

He argued with himself all the way home until he realized that he knew perfectly well what the right thing to do was. The only question was whether he could do it.

In the living room, his father was sitting in his chair, his newspaper on his lap. Jeremy hadn't really looked at him for a long time. God, he looked old. Maybe it had just been a very tough day.

"Well?" his father said.

"I'm not sure."

"Do you want to talk any more about it?"

"No. I'm going to leave it alone for awhile."

"That's a good idea."

The silence became uncomfortable, and he went to his room. He put on a new Rolling Stones album. Loud. Very loud. He didn't expect any complaint from the living room, and there wasn't any.

chapter 22

"He won't do it," Hershey said, spreading the butter
thickly on his roll. "I can't tell you not to worry, but
he won't do it."

"What makes you so sure?"

"You would have seen signs before. You have to be a
fanatic to do something like this, and you don't become
a fanatic overnight. He's playing a part. Like we did.
Remember? We were going to take over the Socialist
Party and make victories. We'd give our lives, our whole

lives to the party, but meanwhile we were studying, and not for the party. We were taking out girls who didn't know Marx from Stalin but were nicely curved. We had daydreams, but where it counted, we were sensible. The nuts you could tell. They went to all the meetings, they read all the right books, the girls they took out had to pass political tests and so they were all homely. And where are they today? Teddy thrown out of his own union because it wasn't democratic enough for him, working in some crummy job, and still going to all those meetings and discussions. Willie, the idealist—you gotta make your life relevant, every third word from him was 'relevant'—teaching in Bedford-Stuyvesant last I heard. I saw him two years ago. He's all dried up but that light is still in his eyes, that crazy light. Have you seen that light in your boy's eyes?"

"No."

"Then you've got nothing to worry about. Of course, you've got to worry, you're a father, but underneath the worrying, don't worry."

"I don't know. Maybe there are different signs now, things you can't see until it's happened, until he does something that makes you know he's a fanatic."

"Not likely. I tell you, the light's there or it's not. You never had it and I never had it, and that's why we made it."

Sam looked at Hershey's suit, one of six he'd bought in London last year, and he remembered the brown leather jacket Hershey always had on in high school.

"Poor bastards," Hershey signaled the waiter, "those

with the light. Sooner or later it hits them, in their crummy apartments or on a cold, cloudy day. It wasn't worth it. They've got nothing to show for it. They won't tell you that, but they know it. They live in the Bronx and you live on the East Side and that eats them up. You spend ten dollars without thinking about it, and they have to think about it hard, and that eats them up. There is no salvation, just comfort. And the more comfort, the better."

"But that's our generation, because we didn't have comfort. Our kids knew nothing but comfort; it doesn't mean to them what it means to us."

"Nonsense. With a few maybe you're right, but the rest, it's in their blood. Our kids may play a few parts from time to time, but they're not going to sacrifice much, and even then not for very long. Look at Russia. Same thing's happening there. That's what the old revolutionaries are afraid of in China. And they're damn right."

"Last time you were worrying about Lila."

"I still am, but she's not going to do anything crazy. And once she gets past her teens, comfort will keep her safe. No, sir, nothing beats comfort. Your boy knows that. Inside he knows it. And that's why he won't do that foolish thing. Ah, comfort. Even saying the word feels good. I must try that. When the pressure's on, I'm going to stop and say comfort a few times. Say it slowly and savor the word. Comfort. Hmmmm. It's like eating something good. Comfort. Say it, Sam."

He said it, and it did feel good. Sam leaned back and

said it again. "You should have been a faith healer, Hershey."

"What is, is. If you're comfortable, why not be comfortable?" Getting up, they both laughed, so loudly that a group of men at the next table stared at them.

"Comfort." Hershey nodded his head. "Com-fort. What a delicious word."

chapter 23

"How come you coming?" Criss sniffed at Jeremy. "You're a dropout."

"He still may change his mind," said Mike, "and anyway I asked him along."

Criss sniffed again and walked ahead.

"It makes sense," Mike bit into a candy bar. "We really ought to see what their regular school is like. It might help in our sessions with them. I wish we could sit in on classes, but that would put the teachers uptight.

Even this way though we ought to be able to get the feel of the place."

Turning the corner, Jeremy saw the school. Big, wide and ugly. "Is there anything more disgusting," he turned to Mike, "than yellow bricks? A whole building of yellow bricks."

"Dig," Mike pointed, "dig the bars on the windows on the first floor."

O'Connor, Harkness, and the six other kids in the tutorial project were waiting for them at the top of the stairs.

"Remember," said Harkness, "you may get some resentment."

"And damned well deserved." Criss was in her Malcolm X bag, Jeremy saw. Early Malcolm X.

"But react," Harkness said, ignoring her. "Don't just be punching bags. If you feel something, say it."

"There should be more interaction between us and them," O'Connor had insisted, "than the tutorial. There ought to be things we can do together as equals."

They were to meet a representative group of them—whatever that meant—in the library. Them were making a hell of a lot of noise in the hall. Them teachers as well as them kids.

"These halls are not for loitering," a fat, gray-haired lady was snapping at a hulking Negro boy. "Where's your class, where's your class?"

"I'm gettin there," he looked down, imperturbable, at the agitated lady.

"Then GET there!"

"Yes, mother," he drawled.

"WHAT did you say?"

"You so motherly, Miss Pierce, it just slipped out that way."

She stalked away and he grinned after her.

Two boys, sauntering along, whooped with laughter at something a companion had just told them, and from the very end of the hall came a shout, "YOU COME ONE STEP NEARER, MELON HEAD, AND YOU GONNA GO HOME IN PIECES!"

The library was large and inviting. Brightly colored dust jackets, posters and literary maps filled most of the spaces between the bookshelves. Several tables had been pulled together in the center of the room to make one long table. Ten of them and two of their teachers were already seated. The kids were mostly black, with a couple of Puerto Ricans and an Italian. One of the teachers, a crisp, middle-aged Negro woman, smiled institutionally at the visitors. The white man beside her, tall, serious and brisk, made the introductions all around. The smiler was Mrs. Wilson, the efficiency man was Mr. Stein. The kids' names blurred in Jeremy's head.

O'Connor started off by suggesting a rotating series of basketball games between the two schools, and maybe later some baseball.

"I doubt very much that regulations would permit that," said Stein.

"Oh I don't mean anything formal," O'Connor answered. "It would all be voluntary."

Stein shrugged, and Mrs. Wilson carefully put the

idea down in a notebook. "I'd like to know what the students themselves have in mind," said Harkness.

There was silence from them. "Well," Mike cleared his throat, "I think that together we could be a great service to this neighborhood by setting up some draft-counseling. I mean, there are legitimate ways in which guys who don't want to go don't have to. Some guys might be conscientious objectors without, in a sense, knowing how to go about saying they are. And there are dependency deferments. And there are some people who might have quite legitimate medical reasons for deferment that might slip by in the kind of examinations they give."

Mrs. Wilson wasn't writing a thing.

"Impossible." Stein rapped a pencil on the table. "That is certainly not the function of a school."

"Again," O'Connor was being deliberately mild, "this could be a voluntary operation with no imprimatur from either school."

A lanky Negro boy leaned forward. "Yeah. I like that idea. Myself, I'm too sensitive to be with all that shooting and bombing." He and several others on their side of the table laughed.

"I suppose that's all right for them what wants it," a burly Negro said. "But man, I'm volunteering soon as I can. My brother, he's a sergeant in Germany, and he likes it just fine. He learned more in that army than he ever did in this place, and he's something now. No, sir, I don't need no counseling."

"You're trying to impose your own obsessions," Criss

said, looking hard at Mike. "That old colonialist thing, knowing what's best for the natives. He's right, he can learn a lot in that army. And he can learn a lot about guns."

"Who-eee!" the lanky Negro pounded the table.

"Nonsense!" Harkness shook his head. "Criss, you're bringing your own obsessions into this. Suppose we forego the ego trips and get down to what we're here for."

"Yes, indeed," Stein said grimly.

"Well," Jeremy finally said, "what is it that we *can* do? Together? I mean, does anybody want us? Do you have any ideas, Mr. Harkness?"

"Yes, I do. I propose that together we study this community. Not in a classroom, but actually go out and find out what the city isn't doing that it ought to be doing. Which merchants are cheating and exploiting. Who the politicians listen to, if anybody, and how we can make them responsive to the community. I think"—he looked at Stein—"we can also study our schools, our school as well as yours, and find out what more *they* should be doing."

For the first time Stein smiled. Sardonically. "To what purpose, Mr. Harkness? To have yet another report, another study? Tell me," he addressed his troops, "would any of you be interested in this kind of project?"

Silence.

"Well," said a plump Puerto Rican girl, staring straight ahead, "it might be interesting, but I don't have any time after school. I got to look after my brothers and sisters."

"Hey," a short, very black boy smiled quickly, "maybe we could do it instead of class?"

"Sure," the lanky one beside him guffawed, "I can just see you investigating, and I know just where you'd be investigating." General laughter—from them.

"I do think," said Mrs. Wilson, "that one thing we could do quite easily together, and quite profitably, is to take trips together. To the museums, to the theater, and share our impressions."

Mike shut his eyes. Criss snorted. Them had gone blank again. Mrs. Wilson was writing enthusiastically.

"We never got back to that draft counseling idea," Jeremy said. "Look," he leaned forward, "would any of you like to do that?"

"Yeah, I see that," said a Puerto Rican. A couple of the Negro boys nodded in assent.

"I can have no part of that," said Stein.

"You don't have to," Jeremy answered, more sharply than he had intended. "Those of us who are interested can get together ourselves. We'll get each others' addresses and phone numbers before we leave. O.K.?"

"I got no phone," said the Puerto Rican, "but I'll take yours."

"Now," Mrs. Taylor smiled, "what about the trips?" Jeremy turned off. Maybe this was the thing to do. Get the 2S, or a C.O. if he could, and help keep as many people out as he and them across the table were able to. Maybe this would grow and hook up with other draft-counseling projects. I mean, wasn't this more useful than getting lost in jail?

"I mean, isn't it?" he asked Mike after the meeting had ended with Stein and O'Connor agreeing to consult further with their respective forces about things they could do together.

"It could be. I certainly wouldn't put it down."

"Then why don't you do it too?"

"We've been over that ground, Jeremy. I'm not going to give them any power over me. They're going to have to take that power. I'm sorry, but that's where I'm at. I am not going to register. I am not going to take that first step. Don't you understand? I'm not going to take their damn card—not even to burn it. I will not recognize that card."

"I guess what it comes down to is, I'm a coward."

"No, it's not a matter of courage. I'm scared as hell. But I got this thing so deep in me I got no other way to go. It's like a call, you know, it's like they used to write about priests hearing the call. I just know what it is I have to do."

"Maybe I don't hear the call that clearly."

"Maybe you don't. You can't force it."

"Maybe I should listen harder."

Mike put a hand on Jeremy's shoulder. "Don't whip yourself. There are a lot of things to do outside."

All the way home there was a terrible lump in Jeremy's chest. He just made it inside the bathroom before he threw up.

chapter 24

Sam left the office early and stopped at Abercrombie & Fitch. Looking at himself in the mirror in the dark brown sheepskin coat, he nodded his head affirmatively. See, it's not too young for you. You're in pretty good shape. Pretty good.

"Shall I send it, sir?"

"No, I'll take it with me." I'll wear it tonight. It goes with the new tennis racket. He felt the lining. Yes sir, you can never be too comfortable. Who cared about him the way he cared about him? Take good care of yourself, Sam, you're all you've really got.

chapter 25

"A very sensible idea." Sam poured himself another cup of coffee. He came through, the boy came through.

"But wouldn't that get you into trouble?" Lillian still had that naked fear in her eyes.

"No," said Jeremy. "We wouldn't be breaking any laws. Counseling is perfectly legal."

"All the same, Jeremy, stay out of it. You never know. What's legal today may not be legal tomorrow."

"Lillian," Sam banged the table, "*you* keep out of it. Know enough to know when you're ahead."

In his room Jeremy started to put on a record, but stopped. He looked at the calendar. Six months. Maybe between now and then he would hear the call as clearly as Mike. No. But maybe.

"Lillian," his father was shouting in the kitchen, "DROP IT! You should be celebrating, not sitting there like a wounded bird." Jeremy couldn't hear any more, and opened the door.

"The boy's all *right*," his father was saying, no longer shouting. "He knows how to protect himself."

Oh, God. Jeremy closed the door again. That's what you think. You won't know it, Big Daddy, but this place is going to be an underground station on the freedom road to Canada. We're going to do all kinds of counseling, Big Daddy.

He looked at himself in the mirror. More talk, Mr. Copout? I don't know, I don't know. I don't even know if I *have* copped out yet. He found the address in his notebook and wrote:

Dear Herman:

How about Tuesday afternoon at 4 for the first meeting? At the luncheonette across the street from your school. Bring whatever guys you can and I will too. I'll also have some booklets and things by then that we can spread around. Please let me know if the time is O.K.

Peace,
Jeremy.

He crossed out "peace" and wrote instead "Yours in resistance." He crossed that out too, and left just Jeremy.